# Adventures of the Karu Mar

By

## R. MORRIS PASSMORE

# PREFACE

There are billions of galaxies just like ours throughout the universe. Billions of galaxies, each with billions of planets, and some of those planets likely have life very much like ours, with land and seas and people and animals (except in the world we are going to visit in this story, most of the animals can talk). Imagine a planet, like ours, where all life was once in harmony, as ours once was. My heart longs for such a place. Just like on our planet, there is goodness and injustice and good and evil in the land of Lusa; with good people and all good creatures trying to make the world a better place for all. This is a story about restoring harmony to Lusa. Captain Eli, who has been chosen to restore this world, travels on his ship, the Karu Mar, to join together those who are destined to fight to bring Lusa to its originally intended state. Jump on board the Karu Mar. Ride along with the crew that joins Eli and be a witness to the adventure. As you read, look for the meanings of the names of people and places; many are from other lands and languages. You can look them up in the alphabetical index as you read, if you are curious. Their use in this story is deliberate, and intended to indicate the universality of the hope for Lusa and for this world we live in.

# TABLE OF CONTENTS

# Adalet and the Umeme

Adalet was of noble birth and ancestry. She was the only child in a long line of kind and just rulers on the island of Chara. For her twelfth birthday, Adalet's royal parents, King Roonaan and Queen Isihe, were taking her on a promised ocean voyage to the island of Doctor Siglos. Doctor Siglos was a protector of all kinds of special and endangered species that found safety and security on his island. An invitation to the island of Refuge was a most special gift, for only those who had been invited were allowed. All who had approached the island uninvited had been turned back; each with his own story of some strong sense of foreboding or some monstrous creature that warned them away.

Many mysterious creatures could be found on the island, and one never knew just what kind of encounter one might have. Some creatures were there to be protected, and others were kept there to protect others from them. One group of nefarious trespassers found themselves awakening back on their ship with their heads shaved bald and their finger and toenails painted with a bright red indelible substance. They had no memory of what had happened to them and they considered themselves duly warned.

Upon their ship's arrival at the island, Dr. Siglos came out to welcome them, and to wish Adalet a special birthday. They were all overwhelmed by the beauty of the island and the sounds of exotic animals calling out, but it was only Adalet (besides Dr. Siglos) who heard a soft, but all- encompassing melodious sound permeating the air.

She enquired, "Dr. Siglos, what is that beautiful music I hear, where is it coming from?"

"What music, dear one? What do you hear?"

"Well, I guess it is not really music, per se. It is a touching sound that makes me want to laugh and cry and dance and dream all at the same time."

Doctor Siglos responded, "Child, if you can hear all of that just now, then I think I have a special birthday gift for you, in addition to the traditional gift I have at my castle. Here in this box there is a wondrous secret, but you are not to open it until I tell you to. Do you understand?"

"Yes, Doctor Siglos, thank you for the present."

After tea and biscuits, and a tour around his castle, which contained more perplexing books and historical articles than one could ever understand, even if one had years to study them, they finally gave into Adalet's polite insistence to find the source of the beautiful sound she was hearing, although her parents still could not hear it.

There was a magical place on the island, the hidden lakes of Eiennoai where the wondrous Umemes could be found. Some believed that all the sightings of strange lights in the sky throughout the world were all due to the Umemes flying in the night sky. The Umemes would emit a mysterious greenish light as they moved through the deep water of the lakes. From time to time, but only at a distance, an invited guest would have the privilege of watching one, or several of them leave the confines of the pools and go airborne. Once in the open air, Umemes emitted a beautiful blue glow all around them as they effortlessly glided about, or took off, disappearing in a blinding flash.

Adalet approached Doctor Siglos, "If you will pardon me, sir, I don't mean to sound rude, but could we possibly, maybe, just go find the music and then go see the Umemes later?"

3

Impatiently, Adalet headed off on her own, for she was sure she could follow the musical sound, but Dr. Siglos told her it was best if she were to just stay close beside him and not wander off on her own.

"Not all the creatures that come to visit this island can be considered harmless, by any means. Let's just go see the Umemes first and I promise you, you will find the source of the music you hear. The lakes are not too far ahead. The ocean reaches under this island during high tide, and that is where you will find the Umemes. They live hidden further back in the cave; they can either move out to embrace the incoming ocean or move through the air out of the cave."

"Well, do the Umemes fly or do they swim, or both?" Adalet asked.

"None of the above, precious princess, they just move wherever and however they choose. They have no wings or flippers, or even a body, they are just pure energy."

Adalet held her gift close and stayed near to the Doctor and her parents as they headed inland. When they arrived to the majestic caves, Adalet was surprised by the size of the opening. It was so small that even she had to stoop down to enter, and the adults would have to crawl on all fours to get inside. Adalet stopped at the opening and asked; "Where are our flashlights, how will we see when we get inside the cave?"

"You will see, go ahead; enter now and we will follow," Dr. Siglos answered.

As Adalet stood up inside, she found herself in a well- lit cavern with a huge vaulted ceiling. The light was coming from the lakes as the Umemes swam about.

"And now for your surprise; you may open your present now," said the Doctor.

Adalet politely, but excitedly opened the box. She hid her disappointment well when she saw that the gift was a simple tuning fork. She had several already from the many music lessons she had endured, even from her early age.

"Thank you, Doctor Siglos," she said, I will take good care of it until I get back home and use it for my music lessons."

"Well, my dear child, you will learn in life that many of the most wonderful blessings appear most plain, and the simplest pleasures are often to be most treasured. That is not a normal tuning fork to be used to find a musical note for an instrument.

Strike it well now, hold it high in the air and tune your voice to the sound." Adalet complied and there was a beautiful, harmonic tone that filled the cavern.

Doctor Siglos asked her to strike the tuning fork again. "But this time, carefully place just the end of it on your chest so that it will continue to vibrate, (yes, I know it will tickle) then let us see what transpires."

The vibrations of the tuning fork, of course, felt strange against her chest as Adalet continued to sing the note. Suddenly, there was a wonderful humming sound responding to the tone that resonated even deeper as seven Umemes rose from the pool and began to circle around her.

The Umemes were the source of the musical sound she had been hearing.

"Now," said the Doctor. "Hold very still, but hit the fork again and sing the note one more time. Seven Umemes encircled her and flew around her. After a brief moment, six of them silently returned to the water, with the seventh coming and resting gently upon her head.

"It appears you have made a new friend. You are the first and only one in recent history to have a Umeme harmonize with your tone. You now have a most-powerful guardian to accompany you and to keep you from danger. As long as you cherish her, she will never leave you, that is, if you want her to be your friend."

"Oh, yes, yes, yes," Adalet answered. "But how do I talk to her, what language do they speak?"

As soon as Adalet asked the question, the Umeme glowed and Adalet clearly heard an unspoken voice in her head that said:

"Hello, Adalet, may we be friends?"

"Oh, yes, yes, yes," Adalet answered out loud. "Yes, but what is your name, little friend?"

"I am called Kagayaku," the Umeme answered.

"Kagayaku it shall be." (At this, the King and Queen, hearing only Adalet talking and not the Umeme, wondered what was going on.)

Dr. Siglos explained to the parents that Adalet and Kagayaku could communicate without words, but that others would not be able to hear the Umeme as she could, unless the Umeme wished it so.

"What a wondrous gift; thank you," King Roonaan said. "Are there any instructions on how to care for the Umeme that we need follow?"

"A Umeme needs no care whatsoever, but a Umeme is by no means a gift any one on earth has the authority to give. The creature is a unique being of pure energy; she derives her nourishment and life from the very energy in the air that is all around us, though we are unable to see it. However, I must advise that even I do not know everything there is to know about the Umemes, except that they are wondrous beings; not to be underestimated, and it would be most wise to listen to absolutely everything this one advises regarding Adalet, for she will only act in her favor and for her favor. Even if it seems counter-intuitive and you or Adalet may disagree with Miss Kagayaku here, always follow her advice and even her commands."

"So be, it, then, Kaga???? Yagu???...well, anyway, little Umeme, we accept you as our daughter's companion and guardian. You are welcome in our family," said the King.

The Umeme glowed several hues of the rainbow and settled down upon Adalet's shoulder.

It pained Dr. Siglos to know that the friendship of the Umeme to Adalet at this time was fortuitous, yet sad, for Adalet would soon lose her parents and her homeland and she would be saved only due to her new friend. Dr. Siglos, who could see this part of the future, could not reveal the tragedy to them. He turned to them and said:

"You are a beautiful family; always cherish the love you share with one another. No matter what happens, know you will always be loved, and Adalet will always be cared for."

Adalet's parents thought the statement odd, but they were wise, and knew that one did not question the words of the even wiser Dr. Siglos.

"Come, let us return to my home for the evening meal and we can share stories later tonight around the fireplace."

As Adalet moved away from the pools, Kagayaku left her and hovered over the water. Some 20 to 30 Umemes arose and encircled her. There was an increasing flow of light and energy that was so powerful and so bright that all had to close and even cover their eyes, and all were unable to stand. They were brought to their knees – not in fear, but in response to the awesomeness of all the sound and the energy. Then, quietly, all the Umemes except Kagayaku, softly returned and disappeared into the pool.

Dr. Siglos and the family left the caves and returned to his castle. There was no need for Adalet to carry Kagayaku, who effortlessly floated along beside her everywhere she went.

Kagayaku told Adalet: "We shall be friends, but only secret friends. Nobody, absolutely no one is to know I am with you. There may even be a time when I will ask you to hide me so that others will not know of my presence. I weigh nothing, so it will be easy, but it must be done quickly if I warn you to hide me. Do you understand?" asked Kagayaku.

"Sure, no problem," Adalet answered.

Her parents thought she was talking to them and both turned and asked Adalet what she had just said. They would never get used to Adalet answering the Umeme out loud instead of just in her thoughts. They would hear only one half of a conversation and could not tell when Adalet was talking directly to them, so it was arranged that Adalet would have to directly address her mother and father if she wanted to speak to them so that her other conversations could be ignored by her concerned parents.

Having shared a wonderful meal and fascinating stories from Dr. Siglos of his travels throughout the world, it was time for Adalet to go to bed.

"You're not going to glow brightly all night long are you?" Adalet playfully asked her new friend. "Do you even need to sleep?"

"I can rest on my stored energy just fine and turn down my glow so you can sleep, which is something I simply do not need to do, but I will not keep you awake. Rest well, for I shall guard over you, my friend," Kagayaku said.

Dr. Siglos knew that there must be some mystical reason for the Umeme to have bonded with Adalet, and he expected it to be related to the beginning of the end of times here, at the beginning of the restoration, to make the old times new again. The following day, he followed the family down to their ship and bid them fair winds and following seas for their return journey. Sadly, he knew their journey was to end in tragedy. He just did not know when.

# The Karu Mar

The storm at sea had subsided; the sky was clearing, and the deep ocean waves were calming. Along the shores, however, the storm surge continued unabated and great breakers were smashing against the rocky shoals and the cliffs. Lusans were on duty in the observation towers on the island of Mekaikki that were built to watch for any ship in distress. It was the last watch, just before dawn. None believed that any ship would dare to approach the island under such conditions, but they were on watch anyway. Suddenly, an alarm sounded from tower one; a ship had been spotted approaching the reef.

Normally, the rescuers would compete with each other to see who could most quickly assemble and launch their rescue boats. Given the adverse conditions, however, there was not so much of a rush as there was debate about the wisdom of launching in such conditions. Who would there be to rescue the rescuers if they were to founder in the waves? In the end, it was decided it was just too dangerous. The rest of the villagers, who had heard the alarm, gathered at the top of the hill to watch the incoming ship, all the while hoping that it would turn back out to sea and out of danger.

There was only a narrow opening in the harbor entrance through which a ship could pass, and then the ship would have to make almost a full 90 degree turn, exposing its side to the waves. In normal conditions, this was achievable, but in stormy conditions, if the ship did not successfully ride the crest of a wave, it would find itself sideways in the trough of the next wave, exposing it to a roll over situation while trying to enter into the safety of the harbor.

As the captain of the Karu Mar skillfully approached the narrow opening, he shouted over the sound of the waves: "Do you think you can work your magic and get us through that?"

"You know I don't like the "magic" word, why do you keep saying that?" asked his companion.

"I know that you know that I know that what you accomplish is not through magic, I just say it to be obnoxious." replied the captain.

"Well you most definitely excel in that area." replied Fred, his companion. "Were it not for the lateness of the hour, we would not be doing this now, but the prophecy clock is ticking, so we must be about our business. *Tend the helm well, and we shall prevail."*

"I do hope you did not intentionally rhyme; you know how that grates on my nerves."

"Who, me? Fred replied with a laugh. "Let's just do this, shall we?

Expecting to witness a catastrophe, the villagers watched as the captain guided the ship through the opening and executed a flawless turn to starboard while riding the crest of the wave that smoothly propelled him all the way to the opening of the harbor. All the villagers were in awe that the ship had so perfectly ridden the wave. The Karu Mar effortlessly made an agile turn; coming about to a perfect parallel docking at the pier, just as the sun was beginning to rise.

Everyone in the village was amazed, and all were gathering to the ship to meet the skilled crew that had been able to achieve such an impossible passage in the turbulent waters, but there was no crew. The captain was alone at the helm. He was dressed in long black boots and a seafaring long black cloak and broad rimmed hat to protect him from the elements. He had no special features to make him an imposing figure, but there was fire in his coal black eyes that reflected both great strength and great compassion. He deftly jumped down to the side of the ship, and as the dock workers secured the ropes, he addressed the crowd of simple, but honest, mostly uneducated Lusans who gained their peaceful livelihood from the sea and the land.

"Good morning to the good people of Mekaikki. I am Captain Eli; I have come seeking a crew to sail with me, but not just any crew, because this is not just any mission. This is not a business venture. Instead, it is a quest of restoration; to find lost treasure, be it stolen by dragons, thieves or pirates, and to restore it all to the rightful owners, for the time of restoration of all things is at hand."

The people looked at each other, wondering what they had just heard. Eli continued:

"Look above you and you will see two flags on my mast– one is two hands clasped in friendship – it is what all who sail with me must pledge to honor – that all Lusans, everywhere are brothers. The flag of the rising sun shows the Old Kingdom will rise again. That kingdom, which celebrated that we are all of one family, is to be restored.

"Fairy tales." one old gruff answered.

15

Another muttered, "Stuff and nonsense, nuthin' but bunny dust."

Yet another commented on the ship's figure head which was a formidable looking angel with strong wings and a stern, but kind face:

"And what about your feathered friend on the front of the ship here. You don't actually believe in angels do you? Such stories are only for children and old ladies."

Eli smiled: "Yes, I definitely believe in angels, my friends. I wouldn't be here were it not for the angels; one in particular."

"Thanks for the free endorsement, friend." spoke a familiar voice from the ship" (although none but Eli heard).

Eli continued: "I know that many of you have forgotten, or no longer believe in the Old Kingdom, but if your hearts are still open and you are willing to make a pledge to serve this ship, the Karu Mar…"

Someone shouted from the crowd, interrupting him:

"Now, wait a minute, what happened to your crew? Did they jump ship because they thought you was crazy? I wouldn't blame them one bit.

And how did you possibly pilot that ship just now?

Another shouted out: "You want that we should sail with you when you just show up here like a nut case sailing through dangerous waters?"

Yet another yelled: "What is this crazy talk about centuries- old religions and an Old Kingdom and you want a crew that will find treasures, only for the purpose of giving it away? What kind of suckers are you looking for? What is your cut and what cut does the crew get of that?"

Eli responded:

"Good questions my friends, but if you are only looking for something for yourself and not willing to join a noble quest to restore joy to those who have lost goods, then I am sure you are not fit to serve on this ship. No slight meant, and none should be taken; your desire for earnings is fair, and this quest is all about justice. All who serve will be paid, but there will be no taking cuts of treasure until we try our best to restore it. Trust in the mission and the promise, and you may serve with us. Seek to serve only yourself, and you will stay on shore and miss the opportunity. So, is there an honest one among you to join me, I ask?"

The crowd murmured, and someone said:

"Yea, we got some folks here who is crazy enough to follow them nutsy dreams of yours, and you are welcome to take them along with you. Take our Sheriff, for example, you can have him. He's always gone on, he has, about soft-headed ideas of pure living and all. He can be a royal pain about justice and rules. And, if all those sea stories he has told us are true, then he is some kind of sailor."

Captain Eli looked around. "Well, good Sheriff, are you there among the crowd?"

A gentle giant stepped forward and stated:

*"On a noble quest, with you I will part, for the laws of my fathers are deep in my heart."*

"Oh yea, we forgot to tell you, he has this annoying habit of rhyming things, he does." someone shouted from the back of the crowd.

Captain Eli privately winced at the very thought of the rhymes, but graciously asked:

"Are you sure you will be able to handle months of seemingly endless ocean and storms and mysterious islands?"

*"Aye, my Captain, I will sail with you, for my heart seeks adventure, this is true."*

18

"Then step aboard, I perceive you do indeed have the aura of a sailor about you: I will make you my Chief, the Chief of the Boat, or COB. Now, are there any others that can endure sailing endless days and nights with him and his lofty ideals? Do you pledge to serve and not to be served, to seek to restore the Old Kingdom? If so, then step aboard and sign on as my crew, but I will make this very clear; if you fail to serve, or if you allow any injustice, you will be set off at the nearest port with whatever pay you may have earned up to that point – no arguments, no free ticket home. Those are my conditions. Who will sail?"

Two mischievous sailors came forward, and one said: "we will take the free ride out to another port, (the other gave him a stiff elbow in the side) I mean we will answer the call."

"Too late, said Eli. "I see your true colors – you will not serve on my ship."

The two slinked away, but only so they could slip into the harbor on the other side of the ship and secretly climb on board. They swam up to the side of the ship where a portal had been opened to air out the cargo hold. They both wiggled their way inside and found themselves amazed that there was so much treasure on board the ship. Just as they were going to stuff their pockets with coins and jewels, there was a flash of light and a great burning flame behind them.

"Away with you," sounded a powerful voice.

Both of the miscreants turned around and then screamed in terror and came running out of the ship's hold in front of all. They looked entirely crazy and they could not speak, although they tried. All everyone heard was senseless, panicked shouting. They ran through the crowd, through the village, and kept running up the hill into the forest.

"Whatever could have happened to them?" the people wondered.

Eli casually responded: "Oh, they must have met Fred."

None had a clue what Eli meant, and none asked who Fred was because they had seen the fear on the faces of the two who had fled.

Captain Eli continued, "Only the unrighteous need to fear – they fled in terror because they boarded my ship with impure hearts. If your heart is pure, there is no threat to you here. Will anyone else volunteer on this noble quest?"

A young father was there with his pregnant wife. They were poor and he hoped to earn some money to support his family. He stepped forward and requested to go.

Eli replied, "No, you must stay and fulfill your duty as a new husband and father. I will return after some time, and if your wife agrees, you may serve, for I discern a good heart within you. Stay and enjoy the wife of your youth and the birth of your child."

An older Lusan stepped forward. He was old, but not weak, and he had fire in his eyes and a calm strength that was still evident about him. "I am called Bartholomew, and this is my son, Barnabas; we wish to serve for the sake of the old Kingdom."

"Oh, the do-gooders" someone shouted from the back: "You can take them along, and good riddance."

Eli asked them, "Do you seek to escape the mockery of these who abuse you for your righteousness, or do you truly look forward to serve?"

"Please, good Captain" replied the thirteen year old son. "My father has filled my heart with stories of his fathers, and we have kept the laws of the kingdom as best we could; please, let us serve. The townspeople mean no harm, they are just making sport of us for being different."

"Come, aboard, both of you and welcome," said Eli. "Is that all? A crew of three?

I thought there were to be six at this port"

A tall, thin, lanky Lusan with what looked like a permanent frown on his weathered face pushed his way from the back of the crowd and spoke to his son, Jeffery: "Let's go, son. Nothing to lose here, anyway," he mumbled. "Might as well go someplace else to be miserable." Jeffery smiled at his father's words, for he knew his heart was not all that glum.

Another in the crowd called out: "Sure, you can take grumpy old Bill with you. But we warn you, he ain't happy unless he is miserable."

Captain Eli looked at him and smiled. "You are welcome aboard, sir, for I can see your true colors."

Old Grumpy Bill lumbered aboard the vessel, accompanied by his son.

Eli paused and searched the crowd.

"Am I not right in thinking that there is still someone here who seeks adventure and a treasure that is more valuable than all other treasures? Did not someone here just last night cry for the opportunity for restoration in his life? Well, this is your chance; step forward or continue in your sorrow."

With that, the blacksmith, an enormous black Lusan whose muscles had been well built by his profession stepped forward and said:

"My name is Panday, and it is I who seeks such a treasure, but how did you know? I spoke some harsh words to my son, Sideros –words I regret, and I must seek to find him and be restored to him. It has been over a year since he took a ship out of port, in anger, and disappeared. Even though I am a black Lusan of a different faith, may I serve on your ship and search for him? My son is of greater value to me than any treasure."

Eli replied: "I know of your people and your faith. Not the color of your skin, nor your different faith keeps you from serving on this ship because I know you seek justice and peace. It is for this cause I have come, to restore all things, even the hearts of the fathers to their sons."

A voice from below decks that only the captain could hear spoke out "So then, another prophecy awakens."

The Captain said, "You are welcome to sail with us, good blacksmith, go and get your tools and come aboard."

"Wait a minute, Panday, you can't leave us." someone shouted at the blacksmith. "Who is going to fix our wares and build tools for us? You cannot desert us. Where is the noble cause in that?"

The blacksmith muttered to himself, "And this is spoken from someone who has not paid his bills in seven months." Panday addressed the crowd:

"I sought to pay wages to, and to apprentice any one of you, but you complained that the fire was too hot, or the metal too heavy or the hours too long, so now there is none to carry on my work. So be it, for I must be about finding my son."

"And I must be about helping you do so," Eli.

"Good Sheriff, please be so kind as to help him load his small anvil (not the big one) and tools onto a cart and bring them on board." The blacksmith and the Chief returned shortly with his tools – and all were hoisted onto the ship. Eli asked the two of them to go down into the hold and bring up a red chest.

Eli addressed the crowd: "As I told you, our mission is to find and restore lost treasure. I have no records of pirate attacks or dragon raids depriving this port of treasure so do not try to claim any, but I want you to see that when the opportunity arises to serve justice for the kingdom, there will always be the means to provide for it. The chief and the blacksmith went into the hold and, using a winch, hefted a giant chest of gold and jewels onto the deck of the ship. The townspeople were amazed.

"All of this is treasure that has been lost and unaccounted for. Our quest is to seek to restore it all to the rightful owners. We shall do the same with any other treasures we find on our journeys. Suddenly, there was a host of volunteers for the voyage. The captain raised his hand and shouted: "Good villagers, when blessings are offered as reward for noble deeds, to hesitate is to lose, I will take no more crew from this port."

Eli addressed the treasurer of the village; "Here is a small chest of gold coins to offset the loss of labor from these who are sailing with me, to buy new blacksmith tools and to train new workers. There is enough for each villager to have one gold coin to commemorate this event. The younger shall have their coin held until their fourteenth birthday. I counted 107 inhabitants, minus the six that are leaving with me – that is 101 gold coins, plus one for the baby to be, and a little extra for additional costs and emergency needs within this village. There are 120 coins in the chest – administer the coins with order and honesty."

And with that, Eli ordered the new crew on the Karu Mar to loosen the docking ropes, and the ship slipped away. Once they were out to sea, Eli thanked them for volunteering and promised they would share many exciting adventures together.

"I want to introduce you to my best friend Clarence, the original member of my crew and the best ship's cook ever. He cooks some divinely delicious foods, let me tell you."

Clarence looked like a typical, though slightly portly chef dressed in the typical white overshirt and a floppy chef's hat. He had a warm, friendly smile on his face and bright blue twinkling eyes that seemed to shine out a genuine joy for living. He ducked into the galley and returned with a fresh batch of delicious crab cakes that they all enjoyed as they shared their stories and got to know each other better.

It was not until the next day that the two dishonest sailors that had met up with Fred returned to the town. They were seen in the tavern – drinking away. One could not help but notice that they had streaks of white in their hair.

"What is that you saw down there in the ship's hold?" they were asked.

One of the miscreants proclaimed that a giant flaming sword swung just over his head – close enough where he felt the heat. The other only remembered horrible glowing eyes burning a hole into his conscience and telling him to flee. Both said their bones shook within them in the presence of something fearsome that was there, protecting the ship's treasure

# Rohani

Rohani was a humble donkey that lived on a small, lonely farm that did not produce many crops, but she did not mind. She was happy just patiently doing the same service that her family throughout history had provided. She was gifted with an extra measure of kindness and compassion for all creatures, and she worked diligently in the employ of the farmer. Sadly, he had become excessively cruel; loading her with too much weight and neglecting to provide her with good food and clean water.

He had become bitter after losing a larger farm he once owned because of poor investments and then by gambling trying to get rich quick. His children refused to work with him anymore due to his bitterness and they left the farm. She missed them; she remembered the happier days when she would give the children rides and tell them stories about her family.

When Rohani could no longer tolerate his abuse, she told the farmer she would no longer work for him. However, he refused to let her go and locked her in the barn. That night, Rohani kicked the door a few times in frustration (and to see how strong it was) and the farmer came in and beat her for her efforts.

Before the farmer left, she pleaded with him: "Please, good sir, I have worked for you for eleven years; you have no right to treat me this way. You know it is wrong to keep me, a free Lusan, as a prisoner."

"Too bad," he replied. "You will continue to work for me until I get my farm back; it is the only thing that matters to me."

"Sir," she said, "that is a sad statement. Your bitterness has cost you your family and your joy of living. Besides, I fear it is not your farm you want back, but your pride, and we are all better off with less of that."

"Who cares what you think? What do you know? You are just a stupid donkey."

With that he swatted her again with a stick. Rohani resolved that night to escape through whatever means.

The same night that Rohani had decided she would escape by any means necessary, another abused animal also completed his plans to escape, for he was seeking to run away from an unjust business partner.

# Sadik

In the land of Lusa there was a beautiful and graceful animal known as a Chimono. Chimonos were rare and charming creatures that appeared to be mostly Lusan. As betrayed by their pointed ears, they were, in fact, distantly related to the Elves, whose time in the land of Lusa ended centuries before. Chimonos stood some three feet high with big expressive eyes set in a beautiful Lusan-like round face.

Sadik the Chimono loved his job, for he enjoyed performing acrobatic tricks and dancing to make people laugh. Not knowing that Chimonos were more intelligent than all but a very few Lusans, they erroneously thought that Sadik did tricks only for treats and money. Sadik was willing to be thought of as just a performing animal because his desire to bring some joy into others' lives was of greater importance to him than his pride.

Sadik had taken a job to work for a delivery service, and he loved delivering packages. He could travel faster through the village than anyone to get packages delivered anywhere. He usually got a treat, some apple or other fruit from the recipient. Unfortunately, his business partner, Huba Amal, got greedy and wanted Sadik to use his dexterity to get into houses and businesses to steal. When Sadik refused, Huba Amal bribed a corrupt official to create false charges of thievery against him. The official took Sadik to jail and kept him overnight in a cold, lonely cell.

Because of their great love for all, the one thing Chimonos were simply not able to endure was isolation from others. In the morning, the official told Sadik that he could either live in the jail cell, or he could be free to deliver packages, but be locked up at night in the home of Huba Amal so he could not escape.

Even though it was still an injustice, Sadik chose being free during the day. Amal had built a small windowless room into which he locked up Sadik each night. However, to try and lock up a Chimono that wants to escape is a fruitless undertaking; their high level of intelligence allowed them to accomplish whatever they set their minds to.

Sadik continued to work at his honest job, and he continued to refuse to do anything illegal. He allowed himself to be locked up each night until he could work out a plan of escape. Sadik had noticed the skeleton key to the windowless room that held him prisoner at night was kept on a chain that was wrapped around the waist of Amal.

One day, Sadik delivered a package to the potter's place of business and innocently asked if he could have a small piece of his best, fire-worthy, soft pottery clay to play with.

"But of course, my little friend." responded the potter; "take as much as you would like."

The following day, Sadik carefully snuck up behind his captor as he was walking. Although there were many other keys jangling there on the chain, Sadik knew the shape of the one that would set him free. He stealthily made an impression of the key to his cage in the soft clay without skipping a step.

Sadik had carefully and secretly held back some of his honestly earned money because he knew his greedy captor sought to take all his earnings from him. In order to complete his escape plan, Sadik took a small gold coin with him and he went to the blacksmith to have a key made. With skillful subterfuge he asked the blacksmith, "Do you think it would be possible to heat some metal and put it into this clay mold in order to make a key?"

Sadik stated that the making of the key must be kept a secret, because his associate could be most embarrassed at having temporarily lost his original key.

"He is a proud Lusan," stated Sadik, "and his business could suffer a loss of trust if people thought he was prone to lose something as important as a key. For your trouble, I am offering this gold coin in payment." Nothing in Sadik's words was a lie.

"Well, we cannot have the merchant losing any business, can we?" said the blacksmith. "I think your little gold coin should pay for the extra work I will have to do. This clay mold is of good quality and should hold up. Come by tomorrow and you will have a perfectly secret copy of the key."

The next day, Sadik picked up the key and was excited at the prospect of his escape. That night while the greedy one slept, he tried the key, and it worked perfectly. Sadik walked out of his prison-room and jumped up to the window to leave. However, when he landed, the coins in his coin purse (the honestly earned money the selfish owner had not taken from him) jingled. Sadik looked over and noticed the greedy captor reach out and grab the coin purse that he kept by his bed. Satisfied his coins were safe, he went back to sleep and Sadik was out the window and off and away.

Sadik decided he would travel as far as he could and never come back. He ran far from town and found refuge from the cold night by climbing into the open loft of an old barn. Not long after he fell asleep, he was awakened by the sound of someone crying. It was Rohani. He looked down and saw the weeping donkey.

Not wanting to frighten her, Sadik called gently from above, "Hey, Miss Donkey, may I ask why you are crying?"

Nonetheless, Rohani was startled and spoke out. "OH, my goodness, but you gave me a fright. Who are you and how did you get into this locked barn?" she asked.

Sadik gracefully jumped down in front of Rohani and said in an exaggerated country drawl: "Howdy, ma'am, my name is Sadik, and I'm wondering how it is you got yourself locked in this here barn?"

Rohani smiled and introduced herself. After she had finished telling her story, Sadik responded:

"You may not believe this, but just this very night I escaped from a dishonest Lusan who also kept me captive. Will you accept my help in getting you out of here? It would be nice to have a companion to keep me company in my fugitive status."

"You get me out of here without awakening that angry farmer and you got yourself a friend," responded Rohani.

"Well let me take a look at the lock that is on your barn door. Be back in a jiffy," Sadik said. In two jumps he was up to the loft window and in but a few moments, Rohani heard the sound of the doors being opened. Sadik stood there grinning as he held a long retaining pin that was used instead of a lock to hold the door clasp shut. "Let's hit the road, shall we?"

As they stealthily walked down to the road, Rohani said, "Sorry to ask, but what kind of creature are you, I have been on this and other farms and have never seen a...a.... whatever it is that you are."

"I am a Chimono, and we are not that common, so I understand. So, which do you prefer, mountains or oceans?"

"Say what?" Rohani asked.

"Well, we have to head one direction or the other, so which destination do you choose for our adventure?" Sadik asked.

"Soooo, I have never seen the ocean; let's go there," she responded.

"Coastal towns it shall be," said Sadik, and he then made an abrupt turn towards the mountains.

"Excuse me, mister Chimono, I mean Sadik, but why are we headed towards the mountains if our destination is the ocean?"

"Elementary, my dear Rohani," Sadik responded. "It is because we must leave footprints leading into the mountains in case someone decides to pursue us. May I have your permission to ride on your back so they do not seek the two of us together?"

Rohani responded, "Your diminutive size is easy to bear. But even if you were five times as heavy, I would gladly carry you in thanks for the rescue. I am in your debt."

"Not at all," said Sadik. So, the pair made an easy to follow false trail up to the mountains, and Sadik had them cross a stream and double back on their own separate trails to further confuse any followers and then he jumped back on the donkey.

Two days later, they found themselves on a hill overlooking the deep blue waters of the ocean. Rohani was most impressed with the sight,

"Oh, it is beautiful; I am glad we decided to come this way. Thank you, Sadik, I think we shall be friends."

Rohani and Sadik continued on down to the pier to sit down and look out at the ocean for a while. As they were watching, a fast-approaching ship came alongside and made a quick turn that took it parallel to the front of the pier. The ship slowed as it passed in front of them.

"Hello there, good Chimono and Donkey, would you like to join our crew?" Eli cried out.

Sadik was impressed that Eli knew of Chimonos. He turned to Rohani to get her opinion. She said, "I don't know."

Sadik responded, "Give us a minute."

Eli asked one of the crew, "What did they say?"

I think they said "right this minute" said old Bill, who happened to be a little hard of hearing.

"Allrighty, then," Eli said. "Come about and have Blue get them on board."

The ship made an amazingly quick turn and drew near to the pier. All of a sudden, two giant greenish arms reached out and grabbed Sadik and Rohani, and they suddenly found themselves on the deck of the ship. Eli jumped down to greet them and asked:

"So, friends, why are you so anxious to join us? Are you some sort of fugitives from justice? If you are noble souls, you may join us, if not this is going to be a short sail. Tell us your tale, and the crew and I will decide your status."

Sadik responded: "Actually sir, we weren't all that sure about this. I clearly said: "give us a minute, and by the way, what were those giant greenish arms that grabbed us? Wherever did that creature go?"

"My apologies" said Eli. "Old Bill here said you wanted to come on board, and I quote, "right this minute."

With an apologetic look on his face, Bill shrugged his shoulders.

Eli told them: "We will get to the greenish arms later, but for now, since you are here, tell us your tales. We will take you back or let you stay according to your will in the matter, depending upon your stories."

Rohani and Sadik told their stories to the crew, Rohani first, followed by Sadik, who finished his story with a question. "Now about those giant greenish arms?"

# Blue

"Oh that was Blue - come on out, Blue, I know you are listening over there," Eli said.

Suddenly, an enormous, (fully half the size of the ship) greenish octopus was before them. Now Blue, as all octopuses, was highly intelligent, but he had such a childlike joy and slow deep voice that he sounded rather slow of wit.

"Hallooo, friends" Blue said in a funny deep voice.

Rohani turned to Sadik and said, "Rather an interesting color of blue, if it is that. OK, I give up, why is he called Blue?"

"Why, because that is his color," Eli responded.

"But he is greenish." countered Rohani.

"But he is most definitely greenish." agreed Sadik.

Eli hushed them and said aside – "just go with it; call him Blue and he is happy."

"Allrighty, then," Sadik quipped. "But, if you don't mind me asking, good Captain, and of course you, Blue, how did a giant gree, uh, blue octopus become a member of a ship's crew?"

"Well," Captain Eli said, "Blue, let us together tell your story. We were sailing along smoothly when all of a sudden, these giant octopus arms grabbed the ship. It was clear the octopus had the advantage of size and strength and could easily turn the ship upside down and sink us. All I could think of was to jump forward and shout at him to ask him if he would listen to reason. I jumped forward and shouted, "Good octopus, why are you attacking my ship?"

At this point, Blue interjected: "They started it, ships would always be shooting their cannons at me just cuz I was floating when they passed near me. In fact, just that morning, this giant black ship full of ugly, and I mean ugly, Lusans fired on me when I was playing with some dolphins. They shot at us for no reason and then they laughed. You know, when you look at things from the other guy's perspective, you can understand why he may be upset with you, and even attack you, and besides, I was *reaally* hungry so I was just gonna ask them for some pickled fish."

"Well, it was certainly more terrifying than that to us, let me tell you, when you wrapped some tentacles around us and said: (and Eli mimicked Blue's voice) "One false move and I am going to crush this ship." The crew laughed heartily at the imitation, as did Blue.

"Eli continued, "So I asked him, why, what have we done to anger you? What will you gain from crushing this ship?" I asked.

"You have cannons to hurt me and you have pickled fish," the beast answered." "I love pickled fish." injected Blue.

Eli continued: "Don't you think it would be a lot easier if we just gave you a whole barrel of pickled fish, already opened, instead of you going through the trouble of crushing the ship and then having to open the barrel and all? What do you say? We will give you the best pickled fish, with no splinters and you agree to not sink us."

"Pickled fish, no splinters," said Blue, "an offer I could not refuse,"

"Anyway," Eli continued, "we brought up a barrel of fish, opened it and actually helped feed the voracious octopus."

"It was wonderful," Blue said. "I could eat my free pickled fish, without a fight, so I decided we could be friends."

"Friends it will be, I told him," said Eli. "You stay with us and we will protect you from other ships shooting at you, and we will buy you some pickled fish at every port. Why should we be enemies if we can be friends?"

"So, I agreed to stay with them," said Blue. "You see, I really didn't have any other friends because I am a giant among them and the other octopuses make fun of me. I can't control my colors like I should, so I don't fit in. But there is one color I am sure of and that is Blue, and that is my name," Blue affirmed.

Sadik and Rohani said, "Got it, Blue, pleased to meet you."

# The Old Librarian

After a few days of uneventful sailing in which the crew continued their training, the Captain gathered the crew together on the deck to explain to them what was next in store. The times dictated their next stop would be on Hang-gu island where an aged ship's captain lived. He was reported to have saved historical items and every chart from every one of his voyages and had traded for, or purchased, even more charts in all of his adventures.

As they arrived in port, Eli paid the docking fees and checked in with the officials. The tax officials were eager to assess the value of any trade items, but they were disappointed when Captain Eli told them that nothing on his ship was for sale or trade. He explained to them that they had only come to meet the old captain, who, he understood, was now a collector and librarian of sorts of all manner of navigational maps.

"You mean old crazy Captain Horace? Ya, he is in the house up at the top of the hill, but don't go to see him unless you stop at the blue house there on the left; it is where his granddaughter lives with her aunt Dorothy. The young one is ill; in fact, some say not long for this world, and if you do not report to Horace how she fares, he will not give you the time of day. Captain Eli, you do know of course, we will have to collect taxes on any purchases or goods you take from Captain Horace?"

"No problem; we always pay full taxes. Thanks for the information about the granddaughter," Eli said. Eli had chosen only Sadik, the Chief, and Old Bill to go ashore. Old Bill was glad to get off the ship for a while. Eli stopped at the blue house and asked if he could see the young one who needed care. The girl's aunt bid them enter. She was surprised to see Sadik and asked what manner of creature he was.

Sadik bowed and said: "If you please, ma'am, I am a Chimono, and I am most glad to meet you."

The aunt then offered them some tea and biscuits. The house was small and humble, and it seemed the aunt was short on food and, therefore, surely tea and biscuits. Still, they accepted, because to turn down an offer of kindness, no matter how small, can deprive the giver of the chance to give.

The aunt went into the kitchen and took the last of her biscuits to serve them. Having politely finished the treats, they all thanked the Aunt and requested to see the girl.

"You must make your visit short; she has little strength left," warned the aunt. The doctor fears she will not celebrate her eleventh birthday.

Eli assured the aunt that he understood and that they were only there to help the girl get well again.

"Please don't talk to me of false promises," the aunt curtly but sadly replied. "I know of her condition; she is weakening by the day and is not long for this world."

Eli responded, "There are no false promises where I come from. Have faith and you will see."

The four of them quietly went into the room, under the watchful eye of Aunt Dorothy. The girl did not awaken. Sadik approached her bedside and began to sing in a soft purring sound.

*"Rest, little angel, just a while more*
*Your healing is coming from a far distant shore*
*Sea breezes are bringing your smile back again*
*Rest little angel, your healing begins."*

At the end of the song the girl awakened with a weak smile and opened her eyes; one was as blue as the deep blue ocean and one was as green as the inland seas. Eli approached her and pulled a perfect model of the Karu Mar from his cloak.

"Hello, Melissa, I have a gift for you. It is said this is a magic ship, and if you turn the sails just right you can feel a cool ocean breeze off of its sails, if you try."

When he gave her the ship, a puff of fresh air blew over her face. It was a cooling breeze that gently fluffed her hair, and a healing fragrance filled the room. Melissa smiled and the aunt began to cry.

"Could you sing the song again?" said the girl to Sadik, and he did.

*"Rest, little angel, just a while more*
*Your healing is coming from a far distant shore*
*Sea breezes are bringing your smile back again*
*Rest little angel, your healing begins."*

Melissa smiled, took a deep breath and gently drifted off to sleep. The three quietly left the room and said their goodbyes. Before leaving the house, Captain Eli opened his cloak and snuck a huge tin of biscuits and a dozen bags of tea to Sadik, who knew to go into the kitchen and put them in the cupboards. Inside the tin were three large golden coins. They then went up the hill to meet the Librarian.

Although it was only a short walk up the hill, the four could not help but notice that all along the path, Lusans were sneaking a peek at them through their windows, or coming out on their porches to see the strangers. None had seen a Chimono before and the other two visitors were quite a sight.

When they arrived, Eli shouted: "Hello in the house. Request permission to enter."

"State your business," came the reply.

"First, we wish to report we visited with Dorothy and Melissa. The child is resting comfortably. She even gave us a little smile before she went to sleep."

"Well and good, then. Permission granted," said an old but strong voice. "I suppose you are seeking treasure maps - are you adventurers, rogues or pirates?"

"Rogues? Pirates? Never," responded Eli.

"But you do have a ship?"

"Well, yes," replied Captain Eli, somewhat perplexed.

As Eli, Bill and Sadik entered the house, they noticed it looked more like a museum than a library. Charts and strange artifacts from all over the world were scattered here-and-there and hanging on the walls and from the ceiling.

"Feel free to look at charts," said a small Lusan whose back was turned to them. He zoomed around the room in a chair with wheels, quickly, effortlessly placing charts here and there.

"Gems are over there, gold over there – dragons behind you, monsters on the left; Whirlpools there in the center," he laughed.

"How many of these places have you been?" asked Eli.

"Almost every one of them, but I would trade them all for a trip to Cockroach Island. Good ship?"

"Say again?" replied Eli.

"Your ship, is it a good ship, able to handle the worst of storms and exposure?"

"Best ever."

"Will you let me join your crew to guide you to Cockroach Island?"

"Well, that depends" replied Eli. "What is your quest?"

As the Librarian turned toward them, they could see his hazed over eyes and knew he was mostly blind. The Chief of the Boat shook his head as if to say no.

The Librarian responded, "There is a healing spice plant that grows on the island. It is the only hope to save the life of my precious Melissa."

Eli responded: "Though the idea of visiting an island called Cockroach is not to my liking, on my honor, if you give me the chart I will go there as swiftly as needed and return with the spices for you."

"Really, what spice? What does the spice I am looking for look like, where does it grow?" asked the Librarian rather pointedly. "Besides, have you ever seen such an island listed on any chart? I have spent my life collecting charts to ensure the location remains unknown. The only chart is in my mind. You see, there is a special plant there, a healing spice plant that heals all wounds and illnesses known to Lusans. We were there once, desperately looking for water or supplies. One of the crew spotted a reflection inland and we went to investigate. My charts showed we should have been on one of the spice islands, but there was no life at all there. As it turns out, the reflection had come from a small piece of sandy soil that had been turned to a thick dome of glass. We assumed it was from a lightning bolt. The area almost looked like a grave site, and all was desolate; but there was a single small flowering plant growing there. There was a heavenly aroma coming from the flower. One of my sailors who was suffering greatly from an infected wound was instantly healed when he but leaned down to sniff one of the petals of this special plant out of mere curiosity. As they saw the wound heal before their very eyes, the others began to fight each other trying to take ownership of the plant."

Horace continued: "I had to draw my sword to stop them. There is only one plant, you fools. If you pull it up by its roots and it dies, that will be the last of its kind. We must only harvest a few leaves and keep the plant's location a secret. Look at yourselves; you were ready to kill for the right to have the power to heal. It is too dangerous for people to find out about the plant. So, ironically, we all made a promise to keep the healing plant a secret in order to save lives. We all took but one leaf each and left the plant there."

"I named the island on my chart, and on every chart I could find 'Cockroach Island' and redistributed them to hopefully deter anyone from wanting to land there. Eventually, we all used up our healing leaves for various injuries and illnesses to our selves and loved ones. The others have passed on; the secret remains with me. I know the hearts of Lusans; more would die killing each other to control what heals than would be healed by the plant. Sad, but true."

I destroyed the original chart that had the name Spice Island so none other could know the way to return. I am the only guide. I do not seek fortune, only one leaf of the healing flower. We must sail today, and keep the plant a secret among the five of us. It is not right that more should die over that which heals. What a curiosity is the heart of a Lusan. The four of you should always consider this."

The crew stared at Captain Horace in disbelief.

"Aaaha!" said the Librarian, "You wonder how I know there are four of you when only one of you spoke? And one of you is but a youth." (At this, Sadik knew that the near blind Librarian had assumed his light gait was because he was a child. He jokingly pointed to himself and laughed silently). "But, I can tell that you still hesitate. Do not let my mostly blind eyes decide for me, for the sea is as much memory and movement and smells as it is of sight. In fact, many times, the sea deceives the eyes. I offer you my entire library now, everything I own. Take it with you if you want, just get me on your ship for the love of all that is pure and lovely. My precious Melissa is my only joy in life and the spices from the plant will heal her."

Eli replied, "Your quest is indeed noble, but given the status of your health, good Captain, in a case like this, I am going to require the crew's support. Each life on a ship…"

The Librarian interrupted:

"Please do not lecture me, Captain; I know the ropes and the rules, and I dare say I have sailed more than you with a more contrary crew than this one, I'd imagine. Vote as you may, but I have seen myself in a dream on this very ship, this Karu Mar as I remember her from my dream, sailing the deep blue ocean, and it shall be so."

"Then let us go to the ship," said Eli, "and we shall cast secret votes to see if your dream was true, or just a dream."

As the Librarian stood to head for the door, the Chief noticed he was also handicapped by a wooden leg. He could only shake his head in wonder, but then he was even more shocked as the

Librarian turned towards Eli and said: " Oh, and by the way, order your Chief here to heft up my travelling sea chest and bring it aboard. I shall not be returning here to pick it up before our voyage today."

Eli smiled and looked at the bewildered chief, giving him the nod to accommodate the surprising request.

As they were headed down the street, Captain Horace insisted: "Just let me stop off and kiss my Melissa," he said. They walked with Horace down to the small cottage but stayed outside as he went in alone. He was delighted to see her sitting up and smiling.

"PaPa," she said, "this funny animal, what was it, Auntie, a mochino? He sang me a song that said my healing is coming from over the sea – and look at this magical ship."

Horace lovingly replied: "Now, now; keep your strength, precious. It is true, we are going to bring back something to make you as right as rain. Rest now, precious child and we will return with the next season," he tenderly kissed her on the forehead, and with tears in his eyes, he turned away with promises to return soon.

"Thank you for the gift and for the ministry to my grandchild," he told Eli as they were headed down towards the pier.

 Suddenly, the Aunt was heard screaming excitedly something about gold and biscuits and tea in her house. Captain Eli smiled and gently slapped Sadik on the back.

Needless to say, the old Librarian caused quite a scene as he headed for the ship at pier side. Ever since he first arrived, the town's people had never seen him head for the pier. When he was nearing the ship, the crew of the Karu Mar looked up, thinking: "now there is an old salt of a sailor who has earned his shore rest, for sure."

As they came alongside the ship, Bill started to help Horace off the ramp, but the old captain did something entirely unexpected; he grabbed the rigging, picked himself up, slung himself over the gunwale and jumped onto the ship, landing with perfect balance. None could believe it.

Captain Eli addressed the crew: "Noble crew of the Karu Mar, this old salty sailor, who is no longer to be known as the Librarian, but Captain Horace, has sought to join our crew. He left something valuable at a place called Cockroach Island that he must retrieve. Hear his story and you may decide by open, or by secret vote, yea or nay."

After Horace had wowed the crew with tales of his adventures, the crew peppered him with questions: "But you are near blind now. How will you find the island? What will guide you? How will you steer past the shoals and reefs? How will you find this thing of value you lost? How long will it take to get there? Are there cockroaches all over Cockroach Island? Who would want to go there?" Their doubts were evidenced by the look on their faces and their murmuring.

Eli spoke: "All your questions will be answered. You may have your say; we will pass the hat for you to secretly put in a vote: aye or a nay on Captain Horace sailing with us."

Rohani spoke up: "Shipmates – the vote is about to be taken – I can sense the doubt. I ask you all though, which one of you besides the Sheriff had sailing skills when you joined? Which of you had sailed through storms and monsters to gain knowledge and courage? Only one of you. Vote as you will, but I vote my life on this good Captain Horace, for his cause is most noble and in keeping with the kingdom. Faith and courage will find a way for us."

A hat was passed for those who wanted to vote secretly, and the tally was taken; it was a tie, which meant Captain Eli would put in the deciding vote. A smile came over his face as he ordered, "Drop the mooring lines, ready the sails, we're off to Cockroach Island with Captain Horace as our guide."

Lusans on board the ship and pier side marveled at the faith or craziness of Captain Eli to surrender his vessel to a blind captain, but Rohani went and stood by his side and said: "Good Captain, I am to be your other leg and we shall be friends through calm and storm." Horace leaned on her solid frame and smiled.

Captain Eli addressed the crew. "Captain Horace is now my navigator; he is to be obeyed in all matters of navigation aboard this vessel. If there are other issues you need to have addressed, my door is open, or the Chief can call for a crew session as needed.

Captain Horace turned his face to the sun and sniffed the ocean air deeply. "Helmsman, get us to the mouth of the harbor and then come about twenty degrees off the starboard bow and straight on until the setting of the sun."

The helmsman looked hesitantly at Captain Eli, who gave the nod, and it was so. The Karu Mar jumped into speed as the sails suddenly filled.

"Funny," the Chief said to himself, "I didn't feel that breeze before the turn." The Karu Mar danced and skipped through the waves as if she were on a full wind. Captain Horace smiled and, if one would have looked hard enough, one could have seen the tears of joy in his eyes.

Just after sunset, Captain Horace called for a sextant reading off of the Evening Star and instructed the Helmsman: "Head straight for her now and keep her directly ahead until she disappears. Then, divide a line equidistant between the North Star and Capella and maintain that bearing directly for the rest of the night. Awaken me at the last watch before dawn; I am going below for rest."

The helmsman was amazed at the knowledge and the confidence of the blind Captain.

As the new day dawned and the crew all got to work, the Chief took a reading with the navigator, and they could not believe how far they had travelled. The crew was celebratory, but old Bill mumbled – "so we are making good time, but where are we going?"

Captain Horace answered. "We need to make good time because of the lateness of the season. Don't be too quick to rejoice and think all will be tomorrow as it is today. What time we have made we may lose to contrary winds if a storm arises."

Of course, that very evening a major storm indeed did meet them. It was a violent storm that raged for three days and blew them off course so that they found themselves in strange waters. Captain Horace searched the air desperately for some familiarity and asked Eli what the charts revealed on their location.

"We are temporarily off our charts, but we shall find our way," responded Captain Eli. "Our mission continues no matter where we are, and who knows what new adventures await."

"I don't want adventures; I want to find the island and get the healing for my precious Melissa," Captain Horace mumbled before he went back below decks.

# Quiz

The Karu Mar was sailing one day on a beautiful following sea when the crew heard another ship in the distance firing her cannons. They could not yet see the ship, but they headed in the direction of the sound to see if they could help. They reasoned the other ship was under attack and the Karu Mar could come to their defense. Off in the distance, they spied smoke, and then noticed the smoke was coming from the top sails of a commercial schooner. Again, the ship's cannon fired but they could see no other ship attacking. As they neared, the lookout spied what could only be described as some sort of a portly miniature dragon that was harassing the vessel. The creature was small, and it could not breathe fire more than 4-5 feet distance, but it flew in and out of the sails on the ship, lighting them on fire.

Soon, the Karu Mar was alongside the beleaguered vessel. They saw the dragon creature (about the size of Rohani) spew his fire onto the

61

ship's sails. It laughed as it flew about and screamed, "You can't catch me; you can't catch me; I am the mighty Margala!"

Blue saw the trouble and swam over as fast as he could. At first, the crew of the ship under attack thought they were doomed as a few of Blue's giant tentacles wrapped around their ship, but he only did this so he could better aim the spray from his propulsion jets onto the sails that were on fire. The ship's crew all cheered as Blue successfully extinguished the fires.

As the Karu Mar was now tied alongside the beleaguered ship, Sadik proposed using a cargo net to snare the beast. They loaded the forward swivel gun with just enough powder and stuffed the net into the barrel. When the little beastie made another pass, they brought it down effectively. Shouts of hurrah arose from both crews as the attacking creature was trapped. The crew of the schooner shouted over, "let's cook and eat the little bugger." but Captain Eli would not allow it.

The Captain of the Schooner thanked the crew of the Karu Mar, saying:

"Well, thanks for the rescue, anyway; you and your strange greenish octopus friend. Never seen the likes of it, we say. You can keep them both far from us, the sea monster and the little bugger if you want; we have cargo to deliver so we will be off and away. Thanks again. Fair winds and following seas to you." With that, the schooner sailed away.

The net was retrieved, and the offender was plopped onto the deck of the Karu Mar.

Captain Eli asked the creature: "Why have you done such a thing? Why would you set fire to the sails of a ship? Do you not know the danger of fire on a ship? We have gunpowder and all is flammable. A fire in our sails could leave us stranded out on the ocean. What were you thinking?"

Still defiant, the Margala replied in a bratty voice "I do it because I can, and to show my power. I am the mighty Margala." With that, it tried to blow some fire, but Blue was quick and sprayed him down, leaving him looking humiliated and powerless. It was then that Blue did something totally unexpected. Blue yelled at the creature:

"And I will show you what I will do to you because I can, and to show my power."

Blue wrapped one of his great arms around the little creature and raised him high into the air, opening his mouth wide as if ready to eat him in one bite. Suddenly, the mighty Margala changed his demeanor; crying like a child as he descended towards certain death in Blue's mouth. Blue kept his grip on him and held him high above the deck.

The Margala cried: "Please stop, I didn't mean any harm, I was just trying to be somebody, to make a name for myself."

Blue replied, "Don't worry little fella, I wasn't gonna eat ya; I was just teaching you a lesson. If we all went about proving our power by scaring or hurting others, what kind of a world would this be?"

"Well, not very nice, I suppose," the Margala responded. I never thought of it that way. I was just trying to be somebody. You see, I am only two years old and I am all alone. I don't know where my parents or any other Margalas are, I don't even have a family."

"Well," Captain Eli answered, "would you like for us to adopt you into our family?"

"Really? the Margala responded, "Oh, would you? I promise to behave, I will do what you ask. I don't like being alone."

"Crew, what do you say?" asked Eli. All said "aye" in unison.

"Said and done," replied Eli. "So, little fire breather, what is your name?"

"Besides the 'mighty Margala,'" Sadik quipped.

"My name is Quizzenrofflesnozinbloken," the Margala responded.

The crew looked confused and some tried unsuccessfully to repeat the name.

"Is it OK if we just call you Quiz?" asked Eli.

"Sure, I kinda like that."

"Well, Quiz, welcome aboard."

The ship's cook walked up to Quiz and asked, "I don't suppose you could help me in the galley, could you? I could sure use an instant fire starter."

"Oh, boy," said Quiz, "my first assignment!" And so, Quiz joined the crew of the Karu Mar.

# The Doradorans

Before arriving at each destination, Captain Eli would gather the crew and show them the chart of where they were going. He wanted all to be prepared for the wonders and the dangers involved. Eli told them:

"Of course, I will not tell you everything about where we are going, or why. Firstly, so as to not spoil the surprise, and secondly because adventures sometimes develop within adventures as part of our mission and one should always be ready to just learn from the experience, not just expect a certain outcome. Too many people miss the joy of living each day while they are waiting for something 'special' to happen according to their plans, and that is a sad occurrence. Give joy the permission to be spontaneous."

Eli showed the crew a map of the beautiful island of the Doradorans. It was filled with fruit trees, wonderful waterfalls of crystal clear, cold drinking water, snow covered mountain peaks. Most peculiar of all, there was a legend that there was an abundance of gold on the island, so much so that there were golden statues of the inhabitants, and even gold that one could eat.

"Gold you can eat?" asked Rohani. "I'd prefer some fresh juicy apples right now over that."

They had been at sea for nearly three months, sailing on a Southeasterly course. Everything they now had to eat, besides the fish they could catch, was preserved or pickled. They sailed for ten more days along the bearing towards the island, but saw no hint of land. There was little breeze and the heat was near intolerable. The crew was ready for some time on any shore, but especially one with shade trees and cold water.

One hot day, during a long boring silence Sadik quipped: "Are we there yet?"

Everyone jokingly told him "shut up" at the same time.

On the following boring day of seemingly endless sailing, Blue interrupted an all-hands meeting by jumping partially on the deck and screaming: "Guys, guys, guys. What do sea monsters like to eat?"

Sadik responded, "OK, Blue, I will play along, what DO sea monsters like to eat?"

"Fish and ships! he replied, and then he doused them all down with water and disappeared under the ship.

On the next afternoon, the lookout shouted, "land ho" and they all rushed to the rails to see the island. As they approached, they could see the beautiful green over all the land, and even one high waterfall cascading down from on high, and their hopes for rest were restored. Not only that, but there was a deep water harbor with a well-crafted pier leading to the land.

Before they went ashore, Eli stated that the crew needed to first re-supply the stores, filling fresh-water barrels and picking fruit to be preserved before any exploring or resting. That work being done, many stripped down and dove into the clear cold water of the river, only to surface shivering. Cold water is best enjoyed as a drink or for dipping, not so much for diving into it.

Eli told them: " Go no place alone. Watch over each other and be back on board before dusk."

That evening, Eli called them all together. "Now, I have selected a few of you to accompany me tomorrow to find where the inhabitants are –

strange that they have not come here to meet us. Panday, Jeffery, Rohani and Sadik, and you too, Clarence; it is time you get a chance to get out of the kitchen and have some adventure. The rest of you may explore as you please, but you must go in twos. Nobody is ever to be alone in magical places; there is danger of falling into delusions or temptations. Not all wonders to behold are wonderful in nature. If there is gold one can eat, Clarence will get the recipe, or we will all carry our fair load to pack some out for everyone. Fortunately, Rohani has volunteered (Rohani crossed her front legs and did a comical bow), so we can load her up to bring back plenty for all."

Eli and his companions headed inland to look for the inhabitants. "I still think it is strange that nobody has come to meet us" Eli stated.

Jeffery looked up and saw a huge mine shaft cut into the side of a mountain. As they approached, they noticed there was a broad road that led right up to the entrance. There was even a welcome sign over the entrance that read: "All friends are welcome, please come in."

The mine was well lit and there was a broad path that wound further and further into the mountain. "Hello in the mine" called out Eli, but nobody answered. As they continued further in, they noticed how deep the mine went below them and how high the ceilings of the tunnels were. The paths were large enough for a horse and carriage. Sadik commented that it looked like one could actually live down there.

As they went further and further into the mine, they saw beautifully carved stones and intricately worked vaulted ceilings, but no evidence of gold. It was Rohani who first heard it.

"Do you hear music?" she asked.

As they continued walking, the music became louder and they could see a brightly lit room ahead where little people were evidently dancing and singing. The inhabitants were dressed beautifully in elegant clothing. It was apparent they had come upon a great social event.

At the entrance of the great hall, there was a beautiful bell with a sign that read. "Please ring and you will be attended to." Panday reached out and rang the bell. It was only a small bell, but it sounded as if all the bells of a cathedral had opened up in joy. All those attending the party froze in amazement at the sound of the bell and all fell silent. As they looked over and saw the strange visitors, they all whispered among themselves.

Some drew back but some hesitantly walked towards the crew.

Rohani walked into the room and said, "Please pardon the interruption, we did not mean to disrupt your beautiful dance."

"It speaks; it is a talking donkey," said one lady.

"Please, good people, allow us to introduce ourselves. I am Captain Eli, and this is my crew. Panday, my blacksmith; Rohani, who just spoke to you and Jeffrey, son of Old Bill here. This is the ship's cook, Clarence and this is Sadik, the Chimono."

"Pleased to meet you," said Sadik as he bowed, and even more people drew back in amazement.

A little golden skinned Lusan, who was about three feet tall stepped forward.

"Please allow me to introduce myself, I am Ororo, mayor of the Doradorans. To what do we owe the honor of this visit to our mines? Have you come to celebrate the festival with us? What brings you here?" he asked.

"Thank you, for welcoming us, kind sir, but we did not know of your festival. We have been at sea for many months and have stopped to resupply our vessel. We are not here to take anything; we shall purchase or trade for anything you deem your property."

The mayor responded: "Those are noble words, but we see you have come armed, and my lookout tells me there are cannons on your ship."

"My cannons remain silent in the presence of the innocent, and we shall surrender these arms to you as a gift right now if that is your wish." With that, each one (except Sadik and Rohani who had none) bowed and presented their swords and musket pistol, handle first to the Mayor, who then waved his hand. Six Doradorans, with arrows drawn, appeared out of nowhere. They all unstrung their bows, bowed, and disappeared again.

"Impressive," said Panday.

The mayor informed them: "Many selfish rogues have come to take from us instead of share with us the simple food we serve. They follow the words they want to hear. No doubt you have heard the legends. People seek the golden statues and the gold one can eat. The gold one can eat is not so much mineral as it is food. The gold is more butter and caramel than valuable. Just a few gold coins are used to dust the entire recipe for a hundred servings. And the statues of golden people are just typical bronze statues of our heroes – golden people not statues made of gold, but the greedy hear what they want to hear. I surmise you are not of that mindset, so you are welcome here."

The Mayor then told the people to all come forward and greet their guests. Suddenly, the six were surrounded by miniature golden people, dressed in their finest.

The mayor continued: "If, you wish to taste of the gold you can eat, you are right on time; that is what is served on this day of the festival. We are celebrating the annual Doradoran festival of the magic foods. It is a pity we cannot serve the exquisite dish of the colors-one-can eat. Unfortunately, the chef, who alone knew the recipe, was lost at sea many years ago while looking for new foods to share with us. He never wrote down the recipe. We tried to re-create it from memory, but there must have been some secret ingredient we can't find. All we end up with each time is just a yucky liquid. We have all the different colored and flavored fruits from the island, but we cannot make them stick to form the wiggly colored food."

Clarence the cook noticed that there was a Doradoran dressed in typical chef style dress and stepped forward to meet him. "Good chef, as the cook aboard our ship, I would love to have a chance to learn any new recipes you could share.

May I accompany you to your kitchen to see how you prepare your favorite foods?"

"But, of course," replied the chef, "and perhaps you have a new recipe for us. Please, come with me."

The mayor then stated, "Since you come in peace, please sit with me as our guests of honor. Let the festival continue, strike up the music," he shouted.

And so, Eli and crew were led through the dancing Doradorans to an empty table in the front of the hall. The music was so beautiful and the dance so elegant that they wished they could join in, but Eli told them to stay seated.

As soon as all the Doradorans were seated, they were all served platter after platter of all manner of exotic meats and fruits. At the end of the many course dinner, the Mayor stood and announced:

"And for dessert, gold you can eat."

What was served was not at all unlike delicious, golden caramel popcorn, except it melted in your mouth and did not stick to your teeth at all. Sure enough, there was the tiniest dusting of pure gold powder on top just to make it glisten in the light. It was delightful.

Meanwhile, back in the kitchen, Clarence had a wonderful time with the chef and even figured out the missing ingredient for their colors-you-can-eat dish. What was lost with the chef who was lost at sea, was the requirement to include ice to keep the shaped forms of the mixed fruit jello from melting in the tropical heat; that was the missing part of the recipe.

When Clarence left the kitchen, he approached Eli and whispered in the Captain's ear: "Get me some ice and we can restore them their festival food. But let's make sure we can deliver first, and then we can save it for a surprise for them."

Captain Eli asked the mayor if the tall mountains inland still had snow and ice at this time of the year.

Ororo replied: "Why, yes on the southern tip of this island. There are glacial lakes and mountains. You do not see them because they are covered by the clouds, but it is an arduous eighteen-day journey to get there. Nobody has been there since the children of our mountain runners no longer wanted to learn the ways of their fathers many years ago."

"Perhaps this, too, can be restored," said Captain Eli. "Thank you for your kindness, good

Doradorans. What do you ask in return for the recipe for this delicious gold you can eat?"

"Why nothing at all, Captain. We will provide the recipe and enough golden food for your crew to enjoy some. How much do you need?"

"Sufficient is the recipe, thank you," said Eli. The Captain then asked if he and the crew, a total of ten, would be welcomed back tomorrow for another visit, at which time they all could enjoy the golden treat.

"But of course, our festival continues into tomorrow. I just wish we had the edible fruit colors for you to enjoy."

"Good, then. No need to pack any treats for the rest of my crew if they can come back tomorrow and eat. Oh, and one more thing, would it be permissible for your head chef to accompany my ship's cook back to the ship tonight? We will return tomorrow with some shared recipes."

Clarence had asked the chef to bring the recipe and a good portion of their colors-you-can-eat powder so they could compare the contents with something similar to what was on board the ship.

"But of course!" said the Mayor.

"Thank you for your hospitality; we shall see you tomorrow at noon," said Captain Eli. "With your permission, we shall leave, for there is much work to do and I want the rest of the crew to return with us tomorrow."

As they were exiting, all the Doradorans were merrily saying good-bye and saying how they looked forward to sharing more of their festival on the following day. On the road back down to the ship, Clarence revealed to the island chef that the missing ingredient for their edible fruit colors was ice.

"Ice?" he said. "For years we have failed with our recipe because of no ice?" It makes sense; when the runners stopped running to the mountains, it was the same time that we could no longer make the dish. The head chef always kept his recipe secret from us. Our dish went from colors you can eat to colors you can slurp. Oh, I wish we had a way to get some ice before tomorrow. To complete our festival would be a dream come true for us all. Ah, but the mountains are so far away."

"Not to worry," said Clarence. "We have a Margala solution that will take care of that for us. I will get the ice and we will secretly make the treat on our ship and then bring it up to the festival to the surprise of all."

"But what is this Margala solution you speak of?"

"It's a Quiz," joked Clarence.

"Well, then give me the riddle," responded the Chef, "I am ready."

Clarence turned to Sadik, who had been following all along: "Sadik, could you run quickly to the ship and call Quiz? Get him the map of this island from the captain's cabin and have him fly back here to us, post haste. Time is of the essence."

Soon, Clarence could see Quiz flying near. On his back rode Sadik, who had already thought ahead and brought some leather straps and some tools to modify Rohani's packsaddles down to 'Quiz size' so he could carry the ice. As they approached, Clarence introduced Quiz, explaining how he could get all the ice needed to prepare the dish.

Clarence took out the map and went on to explain to Quiz that because the Snowy Mountains were mostly covered by clouds, he would have to carefully study the map to determine where the ice lake could be found. "Bring us as much ice as you can with each trip. It may take you several trips, are you up to it?"

"Sure thing," replied Quiz.

"Come along, my chef friend; you and I have some dishes to prepare. The island chef was going to instruct the crew to go and gather fruit, but he noticed that the deck was replete with samples of almost all of the island's produce.

"The Doradoran chef explained: "Well, there is enough here for all. May we use this for the banquet, and you get more for your stores later?" he asked.

"Of course," said Clarence.

It was just a few hours before Quiz came back from the mountains, carrying two 15-20 pound blocks of clear glacial ice from one of the lakes.

"Whoa," said Clarence, "Quiz, I had no idea you could fly that fast and carry that much. Do you have it in you to make one more trip so we will have enough for all the crew and all the Doradorans to enjoy the treat tomorrow?

"No problem," answered Quiz. 'Ice' can do it right now," he said with a smile.

"Aaaaaaaaaah, no puns!" said Clarence. "Get out of here you fire-belching beach ball!" he jokingly said.

Clarence and the Doradoran chef worked diligently slicing fruit and breaking up the ice into several cooling boxes that the blacksmith had made so the jello could form.

When Quiz had returned, and was resting, the Doradoran chef pulled Quiz aside and secretly spoke with him: "Thank you my friend, for getting the ice. Now, I understand that you are a fire breathing being, also?"

"Yes" answered Quiz, "but not like the great dragons."

"That is all well and good; show me what you can do," said the chef. Quiz blew a respectable flame that made the chef jump backwards. "Woah, little fellow, that is more than impressive. That will do, yes that will do nicely."

The island chef said to himself quietly, "Could this possibly, even remotely possibly be true? Am I a witness to the prophecy? I am but a simple cook, but I clearly see this to be true."

The chef turned to Quiz and said: "Now, could I ask that you follow us to the great hall tomorrow, but remain hidden until the Mayor makes a statement, something like: 'It is time to light the festival fire.' At that point, could you fly into the great room and there you will see a fire pit in the middle.

80

You can surprise everyone by lighting the fire and then I will let them know that you are the one that also provided the ice. Let me tell you, you had better prepare yourself for something really special; and it is you who will get the surprise."

"Could this really be true?" the Doradoran chef again asked himself quietly.

The two chefs worked hard in cutting the fruit and preparing the recipe, and storing the treats in ice boxes. Early in the morning when they awakened and the jello was solid and cold and jiggly, both chefs did a little dance of joy.

Before they left, because Blue would not accompany them, they allowed him to be the first to taste the new treat. He was delighted, but he commented that he still preferred pickled fish. Blue said he didn't mind staying behind to guard the ship. They left one cannon charged and ready to fire. If there were an attack, Blue could reach in and pull the firing cord to provide warning. As for guarding the ship against intruders, think of the shock one would receive if a giant octopus reached out and grabbed one of them; they would not stick around, anyway.

By the time they got all the bundles loaded on their backs, (Rohani helped carry the heavy load with additional ice) it was mid- morning, so the crew hurried up the hill. When they arrived at the festival, it was a little early for the big meal, but the Doradoran chef went straight to the mayor and asked him if they could have everyone gather and sit down for a special treat.

The chef addressed the assembly: "My apologies for serving dessert before the dinner, but I am sure you will all understand. Our new friends from the ship have helped to restore something to us, and it must be served while it is still cold."

"Still cold?" The people asked. "Who eats anything cold?" Only the older ones remembered the use of ice in the past. The snow- capped mountains and glaciers were far away from the warm coast.

Once they were seated, the chef ran to the kitchen and ordered spoons and plates for everyone. The crew of the Karu Mar helped in serving the cold colors-you-can-eat treat. All were amazed and rejoiced that their festival was finally able to be completed.

"Oh, this is so delicious, and after such a long time of waiting. Whatever was the missing ingredient?" asked the Mayor.

"It was ice," the Chef responded.

"Ice? Well, if that is the case, how did one obtain enough ice so quickly with the mountains so far away?"

" That was the Margala solution," the Doradoran Chef answered.

"The what?" asked the Mayor?

"It's a Quiz," said the Chef, repeating the joke, and laughing to himself.

"Just wait for the answer until after dinner when I have another surprise for you and for all the Doradorans."

The dancing and celebrating continued until the dinner meal was served. It was a wonderful evening and the ship's crew was welcomed by all the Doradorans, who were especially impressed that the larger and stronger people were humble and willing to serve them.

The mayor stood and addressed the assembly. "This is a festival that will long be remembered. Thank you, Captain Eli, and the good crew of the Karu Mar. I now give the word to light the festival fire. We have eaten the gold you can eat, and the colors you can eat, let the celebration of the fire ring dance begin."

As soon as he had spoken these words, and before the traditional torch bearers arrived to light the fire, the chef signaled to Quiz to fly in and to light the huge fire pit. In he came, and in a flash the fire was blazing. Of course, Quiz had to show off a little, so he finished with blowing a huge fire ring up towards the vaulted ceiling. The shouts of amazement that echoed through the chamber included a mixture of fear and delight among the Doradorans. Quiz then flew down and landed next to the mayor, who, along with all others, was spellbound by the occurrence.

Captain Eli spoke to them all:

"I believe, good Doradorans, that an ancient prophecy has just been fulfilled. Call for the historian to look in the book under the restoration of the Old Kingdom. It is interesting to me that your chef knew it would be so, but the gift of spiritual insight is often given to the unlearned so the learned may learn humility and the need to keep an attitude of learning."

A small, bearded, bookworm type individual grabbed a book that was on the main table and stated: "We know of the prophecy of fire and ice, but we did not understand it. Here it is," and he read aloud:

*'In the times before the restoration, the lost secrets will be restored. It shall be fulfilled by one who comes to you without your invitation. He will bring both fire and ice, and his coming will be a sign to you to prepare your hearts.'*

"But this is a prophecy that has confounded us, this creature did indeed light the fire, but who would be the one to bring fire and ice?" asked the historian.

The chef answered: "Why, it is none other than this Margala named Quiz. It was he who flew up to the mountains to bring down the ice for your colors-you-can-eat dish. And, as you have just seen, he did indeed bring the fire."

There was silence in the room, as the Mayor slowly stood and walked around behind Quiz. He took off his official seal and hung it around Quiz' neck.

"Good Margala, in fulfillment of the prophecy, I give to you the seal of the Doradorans. With this, you are henceforth and forever an honored member of our family. If ever you are in need of refuge, you have a home here whenever you please. The island is yours and we are your people. You will never be alone."

All the Doradorans first bowed to Quiz and then came running forward to give him hugs and kisses.

Quiz thought to himself: "I will never be alone."

The Historian was so shocked he could only talk to himself. "In my lifetime, the prophecy came true. I could never have imagined it. Now, there is so much to do to study the old laws and see that they are all restored in our society."

Captain Eli knew the Historian's thoughts and said: "By the conduct of the Doradorans, I see you all have already done well to obey most of the principles of the kingdom. The kingdom is not so much about laws as it is about relationships and justice, but the exciting part is yet to come as you will indeed see the Kingdom restored in your lifetime."

The mayor called for the music and all then circled up for the dance. The fire ring dance was a marvel to behold, and the Doradorans insisted that all participate. After the dance, Captain Eli addressed them all:

"Good Doradorans, we shall be leaving now, but we thank you for your kindness and your wonderful festival."

As the crew turned to leave, the entire population followed them out of the mine, down the trail, and down to the pier to bid them farewell.

"Come back for the festival next year if you can" they all shouted. "Remember, Quiz, you are family. Farewell, and return to us soon."

From the deck of the ship, Captain Eli shouted to the Mayor,

"Good Mayor, my ship's cook tells me your kitchen was running a little low on your supply of gold to grind into dust. I have it on good authority that ten bars of bullion were stolen from you some ten years ago by a great red dragon that was working in league with the very ship that brought you the bars in trade for dried meats and fruits, and good sail cloth.

"But, how could you know of such an occurrence?" asked the Mayor.

"The elders among us remember the event well. The ship was black and the crew was cruel. When we asked if they wanted any changes to their requests, additions or subtractions, they would only mumble something about being worthless servants to the great master, so theirs was only to obey and not question – under penalty of torture or death."

"Creepy people they were, and there was some short, fat, funny looking young one on board who was watching over everything the ship's crew did. The ship had paid us the gold and had departed when we were attacked by the largest and most fearsome red dragon ever known while we were carrying the gold up the hill. Only one of us was foolish enough to curse the great beast and shoot at with arrows; he was consumed by fire where he stood. The dragon grabbed the gold and flew away.

"Well," said Eli. "I certainly hope we do not ever have to meet up with such a dragon beast, and as for that black ship and those low-life people, we shall be on the lookout for them, also. It is the mission of this ship to find and to restore that which was lost. Please take these ten bars to restore what was stolen from you. Good Doradorans, watch for more signs of the return of the King; the time is coming."

As the Karu Mar sailed away from the island, Quiz stated, "I have this feeling I shall see them again one day. It is like I have some sort of destiny here."

"Well, you certainly have a home here if you ever need one," stated Eli.

# Blueberry Cobbler

Old Bill's young son, Jeffery, who was only twelve was most interested in learning all there was about being a sailor and he shadowed anyone and everyone who had special skills, asking multitudinous questions about what each was doing and why. It was the constant "Why?" that frustrated many. He was so good natured, however, that all put up with him, and many appreciated his sincere interest in their skills.

One afternoon, he was shadowing the Chief, who was at the helm. Jeffery stated: "All I see out there, and there, and there and there (waving his arms dramatically in all directions) is water, water, water and more water. He loudly asked the question: "How in the world can you tell where we are and where we are going?"

Without detailing the intricacies of solar and celestial navigation, the Chief explained that he could use the sextant to take readings by the sun and the stars and keep the ship steered in the right direction.

*"I know my sextant, my charts and the stars. When I am out on the ocean, I know where we are."*

"Well, how does it feel?" asked Jeffery.

"How does what feel?" asked the Chief.

"The feel of the ship under the wheel as you steer."

*"How does it feel? Well, take the wheel,"* said the Chief.

"Really?" Jeffery asked excitedly. "Can I?"

*"Sure, we all might die, but give her a try,"* the Chief said with a smile and a wink as he surrendered the wheel and stepped back.

As Jeffery took the helm, he was surprised at how easily it moved, although it was still a chore to keep the ship moving straight against the wind and the waves as the Chief guided him.

"So, what happens if I see some danger ahead and I have to steer really fast around it?" asked Jeffery.

*"In the open ocean, what would that be? but a drill just for practice sounds good to me."*

The Chief rang the signal bell and assembled the crew and informed Eli of the meaning for the all hands call. Captain Eli explained to them that the ship was going to run some emergency drills.

The Chief instructed them:

"I have explained again and again that on a ship, everything is tied down (or secured) all the time. From time to time, all must be doubly secured against the tossing that a ship endures during a storm or in combat, or in the specific case of this upcoming drill; you all must know how to quickly react to all the loose gear and to secure yourselves from being thrown about during an unforeseen need to rapidly change course when the command is given. Sometime soon, we are going to shout a command 'Hard to port, or hard to starboard.' When that happens, we are going to see how well you have kept everything ship shape and secured. If you are working on something that is going to fly with a quick change in direction, be ready to hold on, but most importantly, be ready to secure yourself so that you are not tossed about, or tossed overboard."

*"If it's not tied down, it just might drown,"* quipped the Chief.

"Now go to your posts and standby for a drill, which could happen at any time now that you have been warned" said Eli.

Bartholomew, noticing that Jeffery was still at the helm stated: "Surely, you are not going to allow the boy to steer the ship for the drill, are you?"

*"I just may at that, and that's a fact,"* responded the Chief.

The day came and passed, and all had almost forgotten about the drill. Suddenly, the Chief yelled out "hard to port" and Jeffery spun the wheel as fast as he could to the left, successfully bringing the ship about sharply. Most were prepared and fared well, but a few were caught trying to secure what they should have already had tied down, and they were tossed rolling over the deck and slammed into the starboard rail, but none was thrown overboard and there was no major damage.

After all was corrected, the Chief assembled the crew and advised them:

*"Not too bad for the new sailors you are, but more drills are scheduled for the Karu Mar."*

The following morning, as a special treat, the cook had used the last of the blueberries to prepare his delicious cobbler. The ship's crew all had smelled it cooking and was eagerly anticipating a healthy helping. None had any idea of the events that were about to unfold.

Jeffery woke up excitedly at dawn and went up to the ship's wheel to see if he could again be allowed to steer the vessel. The Chief was quite glad to see him. The seas were calm, and it was near the end of his night watch. The Chief knew his relief was due on deck within a few minutes, so he told Jeffery to take the helm while he made a few entries in the log. He looked up as the relieving helmsman approached and informed him that there was no pass-down from the night watch, then he went down below to get some sleep. Jeffery remained at the helm with the helmsman overseeing him and scanned the sea before him. All looked well. In fact, the seas were so calm and the horizon so clear that the watch posted in the crow's nest had been allowed to come down and join the crew for breakfast.

The crew was lining up for a warm blueberry cobbler when the ship all of a sudden heeled over and everything and everyone was sent flying hither and thither. The cook, wanting to protect the cobbler, grabbed at it, but it ended up flying over the rail. Trying to pick themselves up from the still leaning deck of the ship, the crew looked upward to see Jeffery at the helm trying to recover from the hard steer.

*"What the blue blazes were you thinking, you trying to give the ship a sinking?"* screamed the Chief as he ran back on deck.

Fortunately, he got there in time to get to Jeffery before the angry crew did. Jeffery assured the Chief that he had taken emergency measures to avoid hitting a rock or a reef that he did not see until the last moment. "Why did you not cry out a warning first?" asked one of the angry crew.

"There was no time," Jeffery responded. "That rock would have ripped the ship apart, I had to steer more than I had to warn you first."

"Well, sorry, guys. I lost the cobbler, and that was the last of the blueberries," said Clarence.

"Ship-ripper rock, my left foot," said Panday.

Old Bill grumbled: "Chief should not have left his post, that's what I say."

"Yup, bet the kid just lost control. Rats, I wanted that blueberry cobbler," said Bartholomew.

Jeffery could take it no more and headed below decks to the sound of more insults against him.

During this time of abuse, Captain Eli stepped up and took the ship's wheel. "Prepare to come about sharply and lower the boats on my order," he shouted. "All crew, keep a sharp lookout for that blueberry cobbler."

"What did the Captain just say?" Sadik asked.

"He said we are supposed to look for the cobbler," responded Barnabas.

"Did his mind go overboard with the cobbler – why should we go back and look for it? Who is going to want to eat it now, even if we could find it?" said Old Bill.

Nonetheless, the Captain insisted, and when portions of the cobbler were spotted, Eli ordered they lower the boat and retrieve as much of the mushy floating bits of cobbler they could and bring it all back onto the ship.

The crew did as Eli ordered, and as they did, they were already figuring out among themselves what he was up to. Having retrieved a lot of mushy bread and crust and gooey blueberries, they brought it on board and placed it back in the serving pan.

Sadik had to quip, "Captain really wants his breakfast cobbler, I guess."

Captain Eli addressed the crew: "Most of you have already figured out what I am going to say, but I must say it anyway. What good does it do to try and go back into the past to try and fix something, or to put it back together? Does anybody want to eat any of this mushy stuff? What is done is done. What I want you to also think about is the fact that the same is true of the words we speak. Take a look at this cobbler. Is it worth more to you than the heart of a young Lusan who needs words of encouragement instead of condemnation?"

"You cannot un-speak the unkindness towards Jeffery you have spoken. He is still below decks, and although he saved the ship and us all from certain sinking, you judged him wrongly and then unleashed your insults. The crew looked up as the talk was interrupted by the voice of Blue calling to them from a distance.

"Yooohooo, Karu Mar, come slowly, ever so slowly over this way," Blue was in the middle of open water, apparently standing on top of something.

Captain Eli said: "Thanks, Blue!"

"Chief, bring us slowly up to that ship-ripper rock so all the crew can see what we would have crashed into were it not for Jeffery's actions."

The crew lined the rail and looked down upon a solid sharp prominence of volcanic rock ledge that was just below the surface. It was the very tip of a long narrow reef that was almost completely hidden from view, for it caused almost no disturbance on the surface at all. Everyone could see that the sharp edges would truly have ripped into the ship's hull and sent them to Davey Jones locker, to the bottom of the sea.

Blue looked deeper into the water and something that raised his interest, so he dived down to the bottom of the sea to determine if some other hapless ship had been torn and sunk.

"Chief, go below and retrieve our young helmsman and tell him he must come topside and face the crew, but do not tell him we know he was in the right. I want him to learn to be willing to stand up for doing right, even when thought to be in error."

"Now, listen, every mother's son of you," said Eli. "Jeffery is coming back topside and whoever does not personally apologize to him will face guard duty on board the next five times the rest of the crew goes ashore. Do I make myself clear?"

"No worries about that Captain," they all agreed. "After looking at that rock, that boy saved us for sure."

When the Chief went below decks to tell Jeffery that the Captain had ordered him to appear to face the consequences of his action, he did not want to come; he just knew that he would be facing more rebukes.

The Chief told him:

*"When you know for sure you are right, and live true, never be afraid of what others say of you.*

*If you know you did right, you never need fear; now answer the Captain's order to appear."*

When Jeffery came on deck, he was surprised to hear the crew all shouting his name and calling him by the title Helmsman.

Sadik had climbed the rigging just to get another view of the rock from on high when he noticed Blue coming up to the surface not too far ahead and waving one of his tentacles in the air.

"Ahoy," he shouted. Blue is calling us over to him – I think he has found something." And, indeed, Blue had made a momentous discovery.

As the ship came near him, Blue informed them that there was a shipwreck on the bottom below; its hull had been torn open by the ship ripper rock. Blue called for ropes to be run through the winch so that he could take them down to the bottom and recover a great sea chest. Blue ran a strong cargo net underneath a great sea chest and called for the crew to begin lifting. The wooden beam of the winch strained and groaned under the load of the chest as it was being hauled up to the ship. Panday, the blacksmith, was called upon to add some needed reinforcement to the winch assembly so that it would not break under the load.

While the chest was being hauled up from the depths, Blue went back down to take another look at the shipwreck. Just as he was turning to leave, Blue noticed a mysterious blue light that was shining from within what remained of the hold of the ship. As Blue peered in, he was surprised to see that the light was coming from the blade of a sword. Blue reached in to retrieve it and brought it back to the surface. Once on the surface, however, the sword was no longer glowing; it appeared to be just a normal sword. It was as if the sword wanted to be found and shined a light from within so Blue could see it.

"Nah," thought Blue; "that is just too weird to think about."

Blue handed the sword to Eli, who was amazed to behold it. By that time, the treasure chest had been loaded onto deck and all were gathered around for it to be opened. There were three huge locks that held the chest secured. Not even Panday could figure out any way to break open the locks, as there was not even an opening for a key. Clearly, this chest was not intended to be opened easily.

It was decided to just leave the chest on the deck until the crew could figure out what to do with it. It was too big and too heavy to be moved into their cargo hold. It would somehow or another have to be emptied, and the contents, whatever they were, would have to be divided and placed in smaller chests.

That night, the crew was gathered around the chest, trying to guess what treasures could be inside, and how they could possibly get it opened. All the hinges were sealed, and the locks would not yield to the best attempts of the blacksmith to open them. He declared them to be unbreakable.

"I wonder," thought Eli out loud.

"Blue, tell me, how did you find this sword, anyway?"

Blue had not told anyone about the blue light, afraid that they would only tease him, as the sword was clearly now just a normal color and not glowing at all.

"By any chance, this sword did not call to you, or anything weird like that, did it?"

One could have heard a pin drop when Eli asked the question, and all eyes turned towards Blue.

"Well, I did not want to say anything about it, but there was this glowing blue light coming from the sword, as if it wanted me to find it, and when I got to the surface, the light was gone."

Eli jumped up and shouted:

"I knew it. Blue, you have found one of the swords of power and someone on this ship, or someone we are to meet is destined to bear this sword."

"Well, don't look at me," quipped Rohani. "Me neither," said Sadik – "the sword is bigger and heavier than I am. Besides, I am a lover, not a fighter," he joked.

101

"Well, nonetheless, everyone aboard must try the sword – I need to be sure. Ensure all hands are on deck, and all hands stand in formation," he shouted.

One by one, they all gripped the sword, but nothing happened.

Eli asked: "Is this everyone? Wait a minute, Bartholomew, where is your son, Barnabas?"

"I don't know," he responded. "Last time I saw him he was down in his bunk, resting."

Eli asked: "Sadik, could you run down there and make sure he is there? You are the fastest."

In but a moment, Sadik was back on deck and informed them, "Sure enough, Barnabas was sleeping in his bunk and had not heard the call to assembly.

"He is coming right up," Sadik said.

As Barnabas reached the deck, he noticed that the entire crew was staring in his direction.

Rohani, who was fond of Barnabas, quipped: "Well, honey, if you were trying to get some beauty rest, I am sad to say, it did not help."

"Not one bit," said his dad with a wink and a smile.

"My apologies; I did not hear any call to order. What have I missed?" asked Barnabas.

Eli was just starting to tell him the purpose when the sword began to glow – and the glow got brighter as Eli approached him.

"It appears we have someone with a destiny among our crew," Eli said in wonder.

"But, what do you mean, Captain. I don't understand you or your magic glowing sword."

"But that is just the point, the sword is not mine, it is yours; it has sought you and found you," stated Eli. "Take the sword and hold it high; point it at the sky."

"Well, if you say so, I will," replied Barnabas, and as he did so, a light shot from the tip of the sword, and the sword swung suddenly and pointed off the starboard beam."

"Bring the ship about on that bearing, Jeffery, and hold that course," ordered the Captain.

Barnabas had just finished asking "Well, what do I do now?" when the sword suddenly swung to point at the treasure chest.

Eli pointed at the locks and said: "Strike them open."

Panday protested: "It would be a shame to ruin such a beautiful sword," he told Eli. "Those locks are made of the most impenetrable metal I have ever come across. You are going to ruin the blade of that sword.

Captain Eli insisted, so Barnabas went to comply as the blacksmith cringed in horror when the sword hit the first lock. The sword cut it open as easily if it were cutting through a twig, and the same with the next two locks.

Eli stated: "This is one of the two swords of power from the olden times. In the hands of a righteous warrior, it will always guide true and it will not fail against any obstacle or any foe. Barnabas, it is an unimaginable honor to be chosen to yield it. I do not know why you are chosen, except it be that you have a heart that always has sought to encourage others. Bartholomew, how proud you must be of your son."

"That I am, but I am more proud that he is of noble character and an encourager of others than that he should be chosen to bear a sword, regardless of its power."

The crew gathered closely around for the opening of the chest.

"Old Bill, will you do the honors?" asked Eli.

Bill tried, but the lid was too large and heavy, so Panday stepped forward and helped. As the lid was opened, the first thing that caught everyone's eye was a beautiful ornate crown which sat on top of millions in jewelry and coins and golden chains. The beauty of the crown was such that it outshined all else. On the crest of the crown were the symbols found on the Karu Mar's flags; the rising sun and two hands clasped in friendship. Beside the crown was a red ruby the size of a coconut. When the light hit it right, one could see a golden star inside of it.

"The beginning of the end and the new beginning are nearer than I believed" stated Eli.

"There are more wonders yet to follow," Fred said from below.

Only Eli and Rohani heard the words, but Rohani, did not know who had said them.

# The Corbatanos and the Silver Mine

While maintaining their original bearings as guided by the sword of power, the Karu Mar had smooth sailing for a few days until they neared an island; they followed along the coast to see if it was on any of their charts. Suddenly, the lookout cried out that he could see someone on the shore; he was frantically waving at the ship as if asking for help. As the ship neared, they could tell he was wearing tattered clothes and was clearly malnourished. The Ship drew closer, allowing them to see five men rush down upon him and put a chain around his neck and drag him back away. Two of the guards fired at the Karu Mar to warn them away. Captain Eli was furious at what they had witnessed. Many of the crew demanded an immediate attack on the island, but Eli responded:

"We must not rush to judgment, but we should all be ready; all hands to battle stations; ready the cannons. Prepare to engage the enemy, but only fire on my command."

All of a sudden, the ship was alive with activity – snipers climbed onto the mast and all was made battle ready. They cautiously pulled into the harbor. There was no other ship there, no castle and only a few guards on a hill who had rifles and grenades at the ready. Eli hailed them and asked permission to come ashore.

"We are not permitted to let anyone ashore except Prince Toh-kali. We are guards. We do our duty, we never question any order."

"Understood, said Captain Eli. Is there a leader with whom I can speak?"

The Sergeant of the Guard answered: "He says he is on the toilet and is not to be disturbed."

So, to be courteous, the crew of the Karu Mar waited ten to twenty minutes and asked again.

The guards responded angrily – "he is still on toilet, go away."

Captain Eli smiled and said: "The poor governor must be constipated. Gunner, fire gun number three into that hillside, maybe that will help him work things out."

"Boom!" The cannon blasted , and the exploding shell blew a hole in the hill. Huge boulders were flung in the air and smaller stones rained down all around. Suddenly, a comical individual in an ill-fitting purplish robe and green bloomer pants came running out of the main tent.

In the confusion, some twenty desperate Corbatanos in chains came up from some mine shafts, followed by their frightened guards.

The comical figure in the robe shouted: "Who dares to fire on the governor of this island?"

Captain Eli responded, "Who dares to chain another and make him a slave?"

One of the enchained miners pushed his way forward and shouted: "Please sir, we are good people who have been enslaved. I am chief Arasibo of the Corbatanos; restore us to freedom on this, our own island that has been taken from us."

The captain of the guard retorted, "Shut up, you, inferior being, we have the right to conquer. This is our island now. Guards get them back to the mines." Under swords and spears, they were led back underground as each one looked long-ingly to be saved.

"Request permission for my crew to come ashore and resupply our ship" repeated Captain Eli.

All right, all right, "but you shall pay for every crumb or drop of water, and you shall pay dearly for this indignity," responded the faux governor.

Captain Eli approached the funny diminutive Lusan and suggested: "May we retire to your tent, I see you are weary of the heat. Let us talk."

The Governor yelled at the guards, "No escap-ing for the slaves. If the ship attacks, drop the gre-nades into the shafts."

He then addressed Captain Eli: "I suggest you tell your crew to stand down."

Eli fired one shot into the air and the cannons on the Karu Mar were pulled in and all secured their swords and rifles.

As they entered the tent Eli asked. "Is it true that you would kill these people if they tried to es-cape?"

"I am the Governor; I obey my orders without question. My orders are that all will work and none escape."

Eli responded, "Has it not occurred to you that if you kill them, you will have no workers? So, what is the point?"

"We have orders that not one is to escape, and the master is to be obeyed. To question is to suffer his punishment, and if you are lucky, you will die before you suffer more."

Eli looked around the tent and noticed samples of silver ore on a table. "So, I see this is a silver mine, how much does it yield per year?"

The governor hissed, "Do you think me a fool? If I tell you, you will try and steal it."

Eli responded: "It is apparent that you are the one who has stolen it. But fear not, I am more honor bound than you to follow orders and my orders are to seek justice and do no one harm except to those who would deny another justice. I ask, because I propose a purchase. You tell me the annual yield of your mines and I will give you ten times that amount in gold to purchase the mines and redeem the workers. That is twenty years of free income at the full amount. Judging from the tailings and your meager samples here, the mines are nearly paid out anyway. Seems to me you are getting quite a bargain here."

The Governor conferred with his accountant, who stated: "You know sir, these mines are almost depleted – they have two more years producing only minimum levels of less than $100,000 per year. To receive ten years in gold would make the wicked one most pleased. Let us tell them a ridiculous amount and see what the captain says."

The accountant turned to Eli and stated: "It is true the mines are old, but we would need $40 million payment in silver = $2 million per year by 20 years. Sadik had snuck around to the back of the tent to listen for deceit, and he heard the dishonesty of the proposal. He quietly pulled open the tent flap behind them, got Captain Eli's attention and mouthed out 5 million, along with number 5 on his hand, but Eli only discretely laughed at him, and waved him off.

"Good sirs, I will give you, right now, 20 bars of solid gold bullion – worth twenty times the value of the silver you seek."

"No!" replied the Governor. "The Master orders all silver from the island, therefore only silver must be used in payment."

Eli responded, incredulous: "Are you serious? Are you so afraid of your Master, that you are incapable of using your own judgment? You know full-well the gold is worth so much more than silver."

"If you had met the Master, you would understand. Nobody changes his orders without suffering for it. Better to be wrong than to disobey and face torture."

"Oh, I have met him – we are old friends," Eli said sarcastically. Your fear of your master and blind obedience renders you a guilty player in this injustice, but I shall get you your silver. I will leave what silver I have and two small bars of gold bullion in advance here while we search for your price in silver. Use this to buy food, tools and fitting clothing and shoes for your workers – surely your master would not forbid this kindness from us as it will contribute to them being better workers."

"Perhaps," the Governor snarled. "Or perhaps not."

As Eli passed the mine, he turned aside when he noticed Chief Arasibo was at the top of the mine, overseeing the treatment of his people.

Captain Eli spoke: "Good Arasibo, please know we tried to purchase you via a king's ransom in gold, but the Governor insisted on silver. We will find it and return as soon as possible to set you free." Captain Eli surreptitiously handed him a small bar of gold. You may secretly spend this for your people if your captors do not use the money I left them to care for you, as I suspect they won't. Peace, my friend, we shall return to set you free."

"Good Captain, I know of a mountain of silver, the lost mines of the Visala, with whom we have traded since ancient times. If you tell them your quest, the ancient ones will remember our pact of peace. Blessings to you, noble sirs. From here, sail north to the Isle of Whales, then turn due west until you reach the sisters and climb to the top of the younger to find the mine. Do not fear the...."

A guard approached and struck the chief. "Go on, Arbozio, (he deliberately and disrespectfully got the name wrong) enough of your ridiculous legends and stories, get back to work."

The crew delivered the gold and silver to the guards and sailed with promise to return. "I will demand justice for the ones I redeem!" shouted Captain Eli.

The Governor smirked and said: "They are still under my master, who may or may not let them go in the end. He is to be obeyed."

# The Isle of Whales

Captain Horace quietly pulled Eli aside and requested an audience with him and the Chief below decks, away from the crew. Once in Eli's cabin, Horace spoke angrily: "Sirs, you know the degree of desperation I feel about my granddaughter. How could you undertake a trip like this to an unknown island that will only delay our objective? I must protest this action and request that we return to finding Cockroach Island."

"Your objections are noted," responded Eli, "but I have two responses: one, that you agreed to join us in our noble quest to restore justice wherever we sailed. Can you think of a more noble cause than what we have just seen? Many of those Corbatanos are in greater danger of dying in those mines much more quickly than your precious Melissa is in danger of dying, I assure you. You must trust, and I promise you, you will return in time to save her. Have faith and you will see."

"Item number two: How do we know that our approach to the Island of the Sisters will not yield some clue on how to restore us on the correct path back to the Cockroach Island? It is a given fact that we are off course, let us see if this restores some clue for you. If not, we shall return as quickly as the winds and waves will allow us so that we can continue our quest to make sure Melissa is restored to health. You have my word, Captain Horace. Trust, for those who seek the higher path will always be rewarded."

Sailing towards their goal of finding the Island of Whales as Chief Arasibo had instructed, the Chief suggested the lookout search for an island that maybe looked like a whale or a group of whales, but Sadik suggested they also be on the lookout for an actual pod of whales that lived near an island, so they agreed to look for both. The ship continued to sail north for six days and the crew kept a sharp lookout all around. "What if we miss the island during the night?" grumbled Old Bill. "Are we just gonna keep on sailing North?"

"Due North, always North until we find it," responded Captain Eli from behind them, and they continued sailing. Three nights later, Rohani and Sadik were up late, enjoying the breeze on the deck of the ship. It was a dark, moonless night, so the stars seemed so close it appeared as if you could reach up and touch them. The Milky Way looked like its name because there were so many visible stars in it that it looked like a fluid stream of stars.

The Chief passed by them and stated: "The sky sure is amazing out here, isn't it? Rohani, I noticed you have never been down into the hold of the ship. I think you could easily use the ramp or we could lower you down by the winch if you would prefer."

"I don't know," said Rohani. "What is down there that I need to see?"

The Chief responded, "If you are one of the crew, you should know every part of the ship you sail on. What do you say, are you up for the challenge?"

"Oh, why not?" stated Rohani. "If I can dance, I can go down a little ramp. Let's do this."

Rohani was more adept and sure-footed than the Chief had thought she would be as she made her way into the hold and looked around.

"Follow me" stated the Chief. "I will show you the ship's storage, then on to the cannon section,"

As Rohani followed the Chief, she saw what could only be described as an angel sitting in a corner. Rohani started to greet him, but he looked at her and signaled for her to remain quiet and not acknowledge his presence. She did not understand why, but she nodded her head in agreement.

When the Chief was ready to go back topside, Rohani asked if she could stay down in the hold a little longer. She just had to speak with that angelic being.

"Sure, Rohani, just call up when you are ready, and we will help you up – but only if you need it."

"Thanks," she replied.

As soon as the Chief was on deck, she rushed over to talk to the angelic being.

"Hello, Rohani, I am known as Fred, although my name is much more complicated than that. Before you ask, the others are indeed unable to see me; you are the only one on board, besides Captain Eli, who can see me or even know that I am here. I am completely invisible to them."

"Then how is it that I can see you?" she asked.

"Once long ago and even in another world one of your kind helped save the life of someone who could not see one of my kind. Because she bore unjust punishment without responding in violence, and you are of the same spirit, you are able to see

117

me, but I will now ask that you take a solemn oath to not tell others of my presence. I am here as Eli's guardian, and my anonymity is needed."

"Good sir, you need no oath from me – you have my word. I am honored to meet you and I feel safer knowing you are here with us."

"Kind- hearted donkey, we can speak again when you want, and I will tell you the whole story of the other donkey, but for now, you best get back topside."

"Up I go," she responded. "Nice to meet you."

"My pleasure," responded Fred.

Rohani was able to carefully make her way up the ramp to the deck. She kept her word to keep the secret, even though Sadik pried her with questions as to why she stayed down there and why it sounded like she was talking to herself.

After about another hour of sailing, Rohani and Sadik were still on deck, enjoying the night sky. Off in the distance, Rohani heard a noise from the water.

"Did you hear that?" she asked.

"Hear what?" asked Sadik.

"It was sort of a huffing sound, like someone breathing hard." Sadik listened for the longest while and then he heard it too.

He shouted to the lookout: "Look low on the water and search for puffs of vapor – I believe there are whales here. Listen and you will hear them exhale when they surface."

Gradually, one then two, then a whole pod of whales – seven or eight, were all alongside the ship. Everyone that was up on deck was excited to see them and shouted at each exhaled blast.

Captain Horace came forward and asked: "What is all the yelling about?"

"Whales, Captain, there be whales here. We are surrounded by whales."

Just as Sadik said this, a whale much larger than the boat surfaced right alongside the ship, with his blow hole right below the Chief. As the great whale exhaled, the COB was drenched with the spray. At the same time, the lookout spotted the silhouette of land in the faint light of dawn and shouted "Land Ho."

The Chief smiled and said. "OK, I think we may have located the whale islands. Drop the sails and lower the anchor."

Captain Eli came up topside to enquire as to why the anchor was dropped. He was glad to hear the good news and stated: "We will wait here until first light, one does not sail without charts near land in the dark. Then we head West at full speed away from this island of whales."

# The Visala

After leaving the Island of Whales and two full days of sailing due west, the Karu Mar approached an island in the distance that had two peaks: one slightly taller than the other.

"The Sisters, "said Captain Eli. "Bring us near shore and seek safe harbor."

As they pulled into a safe harbor, the mountains looked insurmountable. Eli stated, "At daybreak tomorrow, we climb the little sister, the smaller of the two. So, who wants to climb and who wants to stay?"

Even after looking up at the forbidding slopes of the mountain, Grumpy Old Bill, said: "I have cabin fever so bad, I've got to get off this ship, besides some walking might help these stiff old bones loosen up."

Sadik quipped aside, so only Rohani could hear: "Yeah, sure and maybe walking might also put him in a cheerful mood."

After some five hours of strenuous climbing in which they had to cross cold mountain streams and struggle over rocky slopes, they still could not see the entrance to the mine at the top of the mountain.

"Why didn't the miners start digging at the bottom of the mountain and work their way up?" Asked Jeffery.

"I dunno," answered the Chief, *"But, let's keep going, because the more we climb, the closer the mine."*

Even though they were miserable in the snow and the wind, all they could think of was freeing those poor Corbatano captives. As the Captain had said, "We suffer, but they suffer more, and that away from their children and their families, so we keep going."

All agreed it was the prospect of rescuing others that kept them moving forward. Sadik leapt effortlessly from rock to rock, and, pulling alongside old Bill, he quipped: "Got rid of that cabin fever yet?"

"Very funny, Sadik, very funny," Old Bill said with a weak smile.

Rohani had agreed to go along and carry some picks and shovels for them. She graciously carried Old Bill for a while to keep him going, as he was a little older than the others and was not handling the altitude very well. And of course, when it was time for a break, they had hot food and cocoa because Quiz had agreed to come along to help with a fire. Finally, they saw a tunnel further up the mountain.

Once inside the mine entrance they found some old bent picks and broken carts. They tried doing some digging, which was much harder than they had thought it would be. They had hoped to just find loads of silver and be off and away but there was no silver to be seen; only a sign that said: "Seek and you shall find."

They kept digging for as long as they could, but it was time for a break. It was freezing cold in the mine, so Quiz set some old wooden equipment on fire in a pit Sadik had made out of rocks. As the fire blazed, they noticed two things; one, a popping sound that shattered the rocks into pieces, and two, little streams of silver melting from the rock chips. It showed there was silver, but they would not be able to process enough to pay millions in ransom.

Eli had an idea for Quiz to blast the rocks on the walls so that the hot air could break up the cold rocks as in the fire pit, but still, there was not enough silver. They sat and rested, and then went deeper into the mine, where they found another sign that again said: 'Seek, and ye shall find'.

"Well, ain't that what we've been doing all day?" grumbled Old Bill.

"No, that sign is a sign," said Sadik.

"That's Brilliant, Sadik" quipped Panday. "And that rock is a rock."

"No," Sadik said. "It is a sign for us to follow. Quiz, try blasting the rocks right behind the sign that says 'seek and ye shall find'." Quiz blasted and all of a sudden, an entire rock wall just simply caved in. Behind the wall was a door that was locked with a gigantic mechanism. On the door was another sign that said: 'Ask and it shall be given.'

They tried commands like: 'open door', 'door be opened', 'let me in' – nothing worked. Again, it was Sadik who figured it out. He knocked on the door and simply said, "may we have some silver, please?" There was a tremendous noise of rocks being moved and the ground around them quaked. But instead of the door opening, a wall closed in behind them, locking them in.

Four gigantic, resonant voices called out in harmony: "State your purpose, trespassers"

Captain Eli said "We have come seeking silver..." This statement was interrupted by the sound of

The wall moving closer in to crush them. Eli continued:

"But we seek this silver to ransom good Corbatanos who are being held captive, I promise on my honor. Chief Arasibo sends his greetings. I was told your people were friends once upon a time in history. They have been captured and imprisoned on their own island and forced to work the silver mines. Chief Arasibo stated that you would help us to redeem them with silver from your mines."

There was murmuring among the four and they replied in chorus:

"Your honor shall be tested - you must leave a hostage and return to us tomorrow to reclaim him if you care and if you dare. Now return to your ship and save yourselves, but you must leave a hostage in exchange for your freedom."

Rohani stepped forward – "kind sirs I am a humble but strong donkey and I will serve you the rest of my days in this mine if that is what you wish, but let my friends go."

"It is decided," said the voices. Suddenly, another stone wall came out of the side of the mine and everyone but Rohani was on the other side of it.

"It is a full day's journey down, and a full day to return" said Captain Eli, "we must hurry."

One would think that the climb down a steep mountain would be easier than the climb up, but this is not the case. One's forward momentum on the downslope must constantly be arrested to keep you from going down too fast, and it is exhausting. The crew had not an ounce of energy remaining by the time they returned to the ship.

Once back on board, Eli gathered the crew together. He knew the test was to see if they would desert Rohani and flee, or if they would return for her. None could think of having the strength to climb the hill but, for Rohani, they would do it.

As the group looked around, Sadik was not among them. They had been so tired coming down the hill, they thought he was just behind them. He had tried to hide in the cave, but he was caught.

The voices spoke: "Good Chimono, all must go, and all must return. Flee if you must, for doom will fall if you fail, but you must leave."

Sadik was late in coming down the hill, and he repeated the Visala's warning of doom for failure when he was welcomed back on board.

Early in the morning, even before sunrise, they were already awake and packed to return to rescue Rohani. Suddenly, there in the faint light of dawn, the watch called out, "Trouble on the water."

All the crew rushed to the rails in time to see giant bubbles coming from below; bubbles so large that they were lifting the ship. As they watched, four giant beings arose out of the harbor and surrounded the ship. The giants were beautiful in form, with long wavy hair. Each giant was of a distinct race, yet they all lived and spoke as one. They were clearly not some sort of dull giant troll or dim-witted giant.

"We have captured an animal from those worthless miners in the cave and we are here to sell this donkey for gold. What will you pay for this donkey?"

"Good giants, name your price for we will pay all we have and return with more if we are lacking." Eli was going to wave the crew down into the hold to get the gold, but they had already rushed down there. The cook brought out his silverware and everyone took off his earrings or his golden medallion and laid it before the giants.

"You would give all you have to rescue a donkey?" one of the giants asked.

"Yes, good sirs, for life and friendship are more to us than anything else. But we beg your freedom to hurry back to the top of the mountain to inform the silver miners we have still fulfilled our vow to return to them."

"Then, having gained your freedom you would subject yourselves to the ordeal of climbing that mountain again only in order to show you would honor your word?"

Great thunderous laughter echoed across the mountain and over the sea. The laughter of the Visala was so loud that the crew fell to the deck and covered their ears.

"Do you not recognize our voices?" the giants said. "We are the miners you heard from behind the stone walls, and here is your Rohani, though we would love to keep her - she is precious."

One giant gently set Rohani on board and she bowed jokingly and said "TADAA". Immediately, Sadik ran forward to hug her.

The giants then went under water and quickly returned with huge chests full of silver coins and ingots. One of the chests contained intricate silver chain mail and beautiful jewelry.

"We trust this will redeem our captive friends, Chief Arasibo and the Corbatano people. Oh, and Captain Horace, your Cockroach Islands are North by North East of the northernmost point of the island of the Corbatanos, so you will lose no time delivering this ransom. Sail for three days and nights with the third star of Capricorn as your guide. Peace be with you on your journey."

"And peace be with you," the crew replied.

With that, the giant beings began to sing in perfect harmony:

*"These mines they go for miles and miles, Deeper under the sea*
*And there are treasures yet unknown that we shall let you see.*
*Of treasures, wonders, we have more*
*Our friends are welcome on our shore*
*But warn all those who have cruel been*

*That they'll never reach their home again.*
*Following seas and fairest winds be with you now, our*
*honored friends.*

The giants went under the water but two of them surfaced again quickly –each one holding the corner of a huge net in which Blue was struggling. One of the giants said laughingly:

"Oh, and we give you back your 'guard dog' octopus – he gave us quite a fight under there. We were going to cook him up for dinner, but we noticed he was just trying to protect you all. Turned all sorts of funny colors trying to scare us, I guess."

"Ya," said another giant, "and he bit me right on me leg." With that, they turned Blue loose, laughed loudly and disappeared.

The crew called out three cheers for Blue, who was most embarrassed, and slid back into the deep water, but not before he heard another call for three more cheers. It is interesting to see a color-blind octopus blush in different colors.

There was no wind in the harbor, so Blue immediately set about towing the ship back to deep water to fill the sails so they could get underway. Captain Horace yearned to get back to the Corbatanos so that they could return to the search for the

Cockroach Islands. He longed to see his darling Melissa restored to health.

# The Black Dragon

The Karu Mar was making good time on the return trip to free the captives of the silver mines. All were anxious to see the people set free. On the afternoon of the second day, huge billowing clouds began to fill the sky on their horizon. "I have never seen such clouds," stated Eli, "and I do not like the look of them."

"Nor I," said the Chief, and there was much murmuring among the crew. The bank of clouds was directly in their path. Worse yet, the clouds became angrier and angrier and took on a greenish blue hue, with lightning flashes revealing what looked like a firestorm deeper inside the storm system.

"Captain," said the Chief, *"I must now warn; we must, by every means, avoid that storm."*

"OK, Chief, make sure we calibrate our change of direction and speed to try and re-orient ourselves. I agree that it is too dangerous to sail into

132

that phenomenon of nature. It looks like our captive friends will have to wait a little while longer. Hopefully, we will be able to make up some speed tomorrow. Get us away from that evil looking wall of clouds."

*"There ain't no doubt, let's bring her about"* stated the Chief, and all the crew agreed.

The Chief brought the helm over to the port side by 45 degrees and waited for the Karu Mar to respond, but she did not. At first it seemed like the clouds moved in front of them, but the fearful reality was that the ship was being pulled into the storm.

"Blue," shouted Captain Eli. "See if you can help us out here. Try and pull us off to the port side away from those angry clouds."

"Aye, aye, Captain," responded Blue and the crew could see the great jets of water that he was pulling outward in order to set the ship onto a new course, but the ship continued to be pulled in the direction of the storm, which was looking more and more threatening.

"Lower all sails," shouted Eli. "Let us see if there is a wind that is pushing us in." But there was no wind.

"It is a strong current" huffed Blue between breaths. "I cannot defeat it."

"Then, pull yourself free, at least," shouted Eli, "and take Quiz with you." There is no need for you to endanger yourselves."

"With all due respects, sir," they both responded. "We will disobey that order. We are part of this crew, and we all stand together. Perhaps we can help later, either in the storm, or to help with repairs after the storm."

"Three cheers for brave Blue and Quiz," shouted the crew. We are all the Karu Mar."

"So be it," said Eli. "In this instance I will accept your mutiny," he said with a wink.

The Karu Mar was being pulled faster and faster headlong into the wall of clouds that looked more and more like a wall of fire. There was nothing they could do.

The lookout called down: "Captain, I don't want to report what I see, but it is my duty, so here is what I see. There is a huge pair of red glowing eyes staring at us from within the clouds. Upon my mother's grave, that is what I see. Sweet mother of pearl, I tell you there is a dragon the size and the shape of no dragon I have ever heard of that is waiting for us and it is drawing us closer and closer."

Captain Eli responded: "Courage, all of you. Take no thought of fighting this thing, for it would only make it angry. Our only hope is a prayer that justice will be done. That is what we live for and, upon our lives, that is what we have sworn to defend. Courage, all, and be strong."

Quiz was terrified of the great dragon, but he hoped he could appeal to him, so he flew off the deck and towards the huge beast.

As Quiz fearfully approached the dragon, he heard a tremendous, rumbling voice: "Return to your ship, brave Margala," echoed the voice of the dragon. "All must be together for the judgment that is to befall you."

The sound of the dragon's voice shook them all to their bones and Barnabas lost his courage when the sword did not glow blue, so he ran into the hold of the ship to hide.

As the Karu Mar was drawn up to the great dragon, all on board were terrified at his very appearance. More of the crew sought the safety of the ship's hold. The great dragon was larger than the Karu Mar; his well-armored, huge shiny black scales were indubitably impenetrable. As he spoke, the air itself shook:

"I sense there are hordes of stolen treasures in the hold of your ship – do you deny it?"

"True are your words, great dragon, responded Eli.

"But the silver we carry is ransom for a captive people that we are trying to ransom. As for the rest of the treasures, they were not stolen by us. I am Captain Eli, and this ship and crew is dedicated to restoring the kingdom. As part of this mission, we seek to restore lost treasures to their rightful owners."

"That is quite a fanciful idea - forgive me if I don't believe you. You are treasure seekers – do you deny this?"

"No, we do not deny that we seek treasure- but again, it is with the intent to restore it."

"Enough of your lofty words," said the great Black Dragon. It is time for the judgment that will reveal the truth or the lie of what you say, and the stakes are the lives of everyone on board. You will be judged by trial. Pick one of your crew to represent all. If he can drink from the chalice of truth and survive, then he shall live, along with your crew. But, if not, all shall die. No one has passed the test in thousands of years. We shall see if you are as special as all that."

Captain Eli stepped forward. "Produce the chalice, great dragon, and I shall drink it to the last drop. No pride, just assurance of who I am and what is my calling."

"Drink the elixir of truth, brave Captain, and the truth shall be known." A great dragon claw presented a huge chalice to Eli, and the Dragon commanded: "Drink, drink it all."

As the crew watched, Captain Eli lifted the cup and proclaimed: "To justice and to the King of Justice I drink with a pure heart," and he began to drink. The cup was large, and Eli was about halfway finished when the Dragon's eyes flashed, and he growled deeply. The next thing the crew saw was that the dragon had snatched up Captain Eli into his mouth. All those still on board the Karu Mar fell to their knees in despair.

Inside the mouth of the dragon, Eli heard an unspoken voice. It was the Dragon communicating with him in his mind. "So, you hesitated for a second there, did you not?" asked the dragon.

"Oh yes, I did," responded Eli. "Treasures have their allure, but even greater by far is the joy of giving than of taking them. This is the deeper truth. So, if you don't mind, I shall gladly finish your cup of truth, but if it is acceptable to you, I prefer completing the task in the open air."

The dragon relented, and much to the surprise and joy of the crew, the great beast lowered its head, opened its mouth and Eli walked off the end of its tongue back onto the deck of the ship. Then, with a few more hearty swallows he finished the draught and jokingly said:

"Meh, could use a pinch more cinnamon; but other than that, it was quite a tasty beverage."

If one would have been watching carefully, one would have seen a smile on the face of the great beast, but none was watching, they were all too terrified at what they had seen.

"So, it is true," said the dragon, I have lived to see the prophecy fulfilled and my soul is blessed. You are the one who is to come to restore the way for the King."

"Yes, it is I," but many are yet to discover this on their own in their own time, oh great King of Dragons. Please allow me to also help you restore justice with your kind, if you would give me your blessing."

"My full blessing you have, my friend," said the King of Dragons.

Eli looked around at the terrified crew. "Where is your faith?" he asked.

The dragon proclaimed, "Well done, Captain Eli. Thousands of years have I waited. Hundreds have died because of their greed, for it is a great source of evil in the world. I have eaten kings and rogues and pirates; you are the first to pass the test. Once we dragons lived in harmony with all creatures and provided help to all. We were the keepers of treasures for all who needed us to keep them safe. All was well until the murder of Mashal."The King of Dragons continued: "In blind, unjustified rage, dragons condemned and punished all Lusans for the evil deeds of but a few, and the unforgiving dragons began to raid ships and villages. At first, the dragons stole from Lusans out of revenge and spite, to deprive them of their treasures. The dragons reasoned that if Lusans were willing to kill them and each other for money, it must be that they worshipped treasure more than life, and thus did not deserve to live."

"The dragons did not anticipate what would happen to them in this process, but bitterness and hatred always lead every being down the path of darkness. All too soon, the dragons themselves began to lust after the treasures, and to steal treasures for themselves. Sadly, this only made their hearts more selfish and yet more cold; so much so that they were cursed to be never satisfied with what they had, and they suffered a craving to always have more. Better is a little with contentment than great gain with sorrow."

"Captain Eli, in light of you being the first and only to pass the test of fire, I know the prophecy and I see that you are the one who was to come to bring the restoration. I give to you the authority and the power to judge the evil dragons among us. Take this bracelet, it contains the Kohatu Wakawa as a sign of my appointment. Know that it will provide you with full protection from, and, with me, full authority over all dragons. All dragons everywhere will be subject to its power and will have to obey the judgment you declare. In their rebellion, all have avoided me and left me here on the edge of the world, but my power is still strong, and they know it. If I go out to restore the balance now, all would be able to locate me and there would be a great war. It is for their sakes that I remain in exile until the appointed time. You, however, can move more easily and under cover, so I send you forth to help restore the rightful place of dragons in this world. Are you willing to accept the charge?"

"King of Dragons, I accept your assignment, but may I ask of you just a small, little favor?" asked Eli.

"Name it," said the dragon.

"Wait right there," Eli said with a smile; "and don't wander off."

"I recognize something from the olden days, a treasure that needs to be restored to its rightful owner. I ask that you allow me to restore it to you." Eli reached deep into the treasure chest that they had recovered from beneath the ship-ripper rock and withdrew the greatest ruby of all time – the fire ruby from the Old Kingdom of Dragons. It had been stolen by the vengeful dragons, lost in later fighting, then lost in the shipwreck. It was believed to have been lost forever. The ruby was hung on a huge light-weight chain that had been gold plated. The chain was long enough to fit around the giant neck of the Great Dragon. The great ruby glowed in the sunlight, revealing the shape of a golden star deep within it. "I believe this is rightfully yours, great King. The favor I ask is that you allow me to place it back upon your magnificent neck, where it belongs."

The King of Dragons pulled back in awe, then bowed his head. Eli climbed the rigging, and, with the help of Quiz, who flew the chain to the other side of the great dragon, fitted it around his great neck. The ruby continued to glow brighter, and the golden star emitted a piercing light.

All the crew gave a bow of respect to the monarch. That is, all but one. Old Captain Horace refused to even go topside; his hatred for dragons was so bitter that there was no room in his soul to accept that there was any possibility that a dragon, any dragon, could hold any value or be worthy to live, much less to be respected.

The King of Dragons stated: "I am honored, and my soul is blessed. I now know the Kingdom is to be restored in my lifetime, which I did not believe until today. Peace be with you, Captain and crew of the Karu Mar, and you too, Fred." (At this, Rohani, the only other one to understand, snickered). As Sadik looked at her suspiciously, she responded with: "What?" in order to counter his curiosity.

"Peace be with you all in all your journeys," the dragon said as he slowly sank into the depths of the ocean. All at once, the ship was released from the force that had pulled them in and they were able to resume their journey.

# The Mutiny of Captain Horace

Each time Captain Horace heard anyone talking respectfully about the Great Dragon, his anger would burn hotter. The loss of his leg, as well as the loss of one of his ships and many of his crew were due to a battle with an evil red dragon; it was an injury that he could never forgive. He had sworn hatred for any and all dragons from that time forward. There was no room in his heart for any other possibility than that all dragons were evil, even if they appeared to be good. Horace's anger, coupled with the loss of time that was causing yet another delay in his search for the Cockroach Island so that he could save his precious granddaughter Melissa, consumed him. "What kind of a leader could Eli be that he could consort with evil giant lizards?" Horace mumbled out loud.

Rohani, who was nearby answered; "Did you not just see what happened here? Are you so blind that you cannot see that greatness is being restored?"

Horace yelled, "Now I am being counseled by a donkey! I have to get off of this ship!"

The Chief, who had heard it all stated:

*"My dear Captain, the truth is the truth, you know of course,*
*be it stated by a donkey, a dragon, or a horse."*

Rohani further admonished Captain Horace:

"Eli is a great leader and a great thing has happened here before our eyes whether you can see it or not. It is never right to refuse forgiveness. Even you may one day need the help of a dragon."

"Good words, and true, Rohani," Fred said from below decks. "You know, I have it on good authority that Horace is going to have to eat his words very soon.

"How soon." asked Rohani.

"Verrrry soon." replied the angel.

"I would never accept the help of a dragon, never." replied Horace. "Right now, I have my own agenda to follow, and continuing on with this crazy ship is not a part of it."

Sooner or later Horace was going to explode in anger, and later that day it happened. Captain Eli had called a meeting of the ship's crew that afternoon to discuss his change in plans. Suddenly, Horace stood up and drew out two pistols and pointed them at Eli.

"This is a mutiny" shouted Horace. "I want off this ship and I want off this ship now. I am taking command of the long boat right now. Captain Eli is under my pistols until the boat is loaded to my satisfaction. You people are all fools to align yourselves with dragons and to go about fighting against an evil prince to free some people who will likely never even thank you a year from now. I am on a mission, a mission to save the life of my granddaughter, and Captain Eli has broken his promise to me. Set me adrift now in the ship's boat with two weeks provision, and I will sail on my own to fulfill my quest for my granddaughter's life. Do so, or I will be forced to take drastic action. This is a mutiny, and you are bound by code to hang me or maroon me. I request to be marooned in the ship's boat as my punishment."

Captain Eli calmly spoke to Horace: "Easy there, Captain, fingers off the triggers if you

please. One careless slip and, then it will not be
mutiny, but murder, and there is no easy forgiveness for that. You can't rescue Melissa once
you are dead, so put up the pistols and we will
grant you your request for the ship's boat, or to be
marooned. I give orders that nobody is to interfere
with Captain Horace while he goes to gather his
map and the ship's boat be loaded with provisions.
That is my final word on this. Eli pointed at the
map on the table. I will accompany him to that island there, where we can talk in private, one captain to another. Do you accept, Captain Horace?"

"Yes, I accept."

There was great curiosity among the crew as the
two captains were lowered away and sailed to a
small island for their conference. Rohani had insisted on accompanying Horace, as she was honor
bound by her word to stand beside him, and she
had grown close to him, but Captain Eli forbade it.

Once on the island, the captains got out of the
boat for a conference. Captain Eli repeated to Horace that the terms were to be hanged or to be marooned. Your honest answer to my next question
will determine your fate. Here is your question:
"If, in order to rescue Melissa, you would first have
to forgive the dragons, what would your answer
be? Which is greater, your hatred of dragons or

146

your love for your granddaughter? Remember, I always know when someone is lying."

Horace thought long and hard before he answered. "I cannot let go of my hatred of dragons, all of them are evil, but I cannot let go of my love for Melissa."

Eli responded: "Your hatred has bled over into other areas of your life, as hatred always does, poisoning your soul and blinding you to what is true and beautiful in other areas. I see only one solution to this problem; consider yourself marooned, but it will be on this island, and not in taking my long boat." With that, Eli suddenly jumped back into the boat, threw Horace's sea bag and provisions on the sand, and left him marooned.

From a distance the ship's crew saw Captain Eli leaving Horace stranded, and all were aghast at the cruelty of the judgment. How could Eli do that to poor old Horace? Sure, he committed mutiny, but he was just desperate to save his granddaughter.

As Eli came back aboard and noted all of the suspicious stares of the crew, he stated:

"I only ask that you do not judge any eventuality without knowing all of the facts and all of the outcomes, which I expect won't come easy to you, but trust, and one day you will understand. Help is on the way for Captain Horace, you have my promise. For now, we have some prisoners to rescue and we cannot be delayed any longer."

Noticing Rohani's deep despair, Eli bent down and whispered into her ear and her burden was lifted as she remembered Fred's words about Horace needing a dragon.

Everyone on the Karu Mar was desperate to make up lost time so they could return and free the captives in the silver mines.

# Toh-Kahli's Treachery

After the family's visit with Doctor Siglos on his island, Adalet enjoyed several months of wonderful visits and peaceful sailing. With the exception of her parents, nobody on board was aware of the presence of Kagayaku, she remained a carefully guarded secret. One calm, beautiful day, the lookout on their ship called out that he had spotted a ship on the horizon. Adalet ran up on deck to see what was happening. The lookout's following reports indicated that it was a large ship, and that it was headed straight on an intercept course to meet them.

King Roonan wondered what ship it could be, but as it drew nearer, his heart fell as he noted it was a huge, all-black vessel. If it were the ship he feared it to be, it could easily overtake them, so there was no need to try and outrun it. As the lookout called down the description of the ship's flags, all hope on board was lost. A black flag showed the red fist and the red dragon; it was the flag ship of the evil Prince Toh-kali.

The approaching vessel did not wait for a sign of a willingness to communicate, or to surrender before it attacked. The shots were perfectly aimed to disable the vessel, and the black ship pulled alongside where it could deliver a final broadside from her 18 cannons and send Adalet's ship to the bottom of the sea; but first would come the boarding and the pillaging of the innocents on board.

Kagayaku quickly instructed Adalet to go to the stern of the ship to be ready to escape out the back windows in the captain's quarters. Adalet did not understand the danger that they were all facing, so she asked to go and stay close to her mother and father.

"Fine, quickly, then, go to them if you must, and do as they say." Kagayaku urged.

Adalet started above deck to find her parents, who were already searching for, and calling out to her. In a flash, Kagayaku appeared in front of Adalet's parents, reaching them well before she did.

"Listen well." both heard the Umeme speak in their minds. "This Evil Prince comes only to enslave, to kill and to destroy. Now, hug and kiss Adalet quickly and tell her you will meet her as soon as you can. Send her to the captain's quarters where we can escape out the window. I will quickly and quietly carry her away, and I promise she will be cared for. Here she comes, now – send her quickly or she will endure suffering."

As Adalet approached, her parents got on their knees to hug her, and followed the Umeme's instructions. "Quickly," they cried, "run to the captain's quarters now! Here come the soldiers." It tore at their hearts, but they knew their fate was sealed. Their only comfort was knowing that their daughter would survive and be free.

Adalet followed her parents' instructions, just barely getting into the captain's cabin on time. She locked the door before the evil soldiers reached her. As they were bashing on the door to break it down, Adalet heard screams and gunfire. Kagayaku flashed before her:

"Listen, open the windows and hold me very tightly in your hands. Reach your arms out the window and get ready. Hold on, do not let go; are you ready? I am going to fly you out of here."

"But what about my mother and father?" Adalet asked.

"If you and I together could save them and everyone on board, we would stay, but we cannot. If you were captured and they could fly away free, would you want them to stay with you or to go free?"

"I would want them to go," Adalet responded.

"And that is exactly what we are doing. Hold on tight, we are airborne," said Kagayaku.

The Umeme took off with a powerful but gentle whoosh of energy, and Adalet found herself flying through the air.

"How well can you swim?" Kagayaku asked her.

"Well enough," she replied, "though I prefer more temperate waters," she quipped.

They were flying about six feet above the water when Kagayaku said: "OK, then, down we go." and they descended into the frigid waters. "We will hide here in the water; they will spot us if I remain in the air. I can reflect the light off the waves to hide us."

Back on the ship, Prince Toh-kali was incensed that he could not locate Adalet.

"Where is the princess, where is she?" he screamed. "No one escapes from me. Bring me the royals"

When they were brought near, Toh-kali pointed a pistol at the queen and said:

"If you do not want to watch your wife die right now before you, you had best call your daughter. If she is not on board, you will tell me where we can find her."

Queen Isihe calmly stated that the princess was not on the ship. "When we were on the island of Doctor Siglos we were warned of danger, so she did not come here with us." (by here she meant right here right now, and thus did not really lie). "Thanks to Doctor Siglos, she has escaped. Of course, if you don't believe us, you can go ask Dr. Siglos. You may go to his island to find out for yourself, and good luck with showing up there uninvited."

"Do you mock me when under the threat of death?" asked Toh-kali.

"King Roonaan, this is your last chance, where is the princess?"

"It is as my beautiful Queen has stated, We were warned of the danger, so our daughter is not with us. But you aren't going to kill either of us, because we are worth more to you alive as hostages. If you kill either of us, you lose a bargaining chip, or live bait, or ransom, or whatever your little evil mind is planning to do with us. Regardless, it is nonetheless a misfortune to be in the presence of your wretchedness."

Toh-kali seethed in anger. "Once your ransom is paid I shall repay you for this insult."

He turned to his soldiers and screamed: "Take all treasures, then burn the ship and scuttle it, but save the ship's colors and seals as proof of capture."

As they sailed away, the evil prince ensured the royals remained on the deck of his ship to watch the destruction and sinking of their ship, taunting them about the loss.

# Adalet Adrift

The next thing Adalet heard was the sound of a huge explosion from behind her; as she turned to look, she saw the black ship sailing away from her rapidly sinking vessel.

"Adalet, I am not at my full strength yet, so I cannot carry you far, said Kagayaku. As the Black Ship leaves, we will have to circle back and find some wreckage to float on. Do not despair, your mother and father were not on the ship when it went down, they were taken captive and your people will redeem them if they can, even at a great sacrifice. At the right time, we have been chosen to play a role in their rescue, so we must keep our courage and remain strong. I am sorry that I do not yet have the knowledge or strength for combat so that I could have saved them."

Circling back around to the shipwreck site, Kagayaku found a good-sized plank on which Adalet could easily stay dry until they could be rescued.

"Once I have recharged, and as soon as it is dark, I will light up the sky and some ship will find us, to be sure. I will not leave you, my friend. All will be made right again. Sadness will flee and all will be restored. Sing us a song, Adalet, a song of hope." Kagayaku harmonized the notes as Adalet sang:

*There is a land, a wonderful land, which is more real than any other*
*Where kindness and mercy rule from the throne, and all may live as brothers.*
*This is my home; I shall return, though I be carried far away*
*Evil may endure for the night, but justice will have her way.*

The beautiful sound drifted across the water and high into the heavens, and the One Source of all the worlds smiled as Adalet lay down her head and drifted off to a peaceful rest.

As the dusk turned to dark, Kagayaku gently lifted away from Adalet so as not to disturb her and then she let loose a blazing, glowing energy as a signal beacon. Though the light could be seen from much further away, any ship within 12 nautical miles would be able to pinpoint the light's

156

location on the horizon, which is precisely what happened as the lookout on the Karu Mar saw the anomalous blaze.

Never before had he seen such a marvelous light. He rang the alarm bell so that all hands could come and witness the phenomenon. "All hands on deck!" the lookout shouted. Many thought this was an alarm announcing danger, but as soon as they hit the deck, they were awestruck by the beauty of the light, and were grateful for the alarming call.

"Now, there is something you don't see everyday," an awestruck Grumpy Bill said.

Captain Eli heard Fred instruct him to make full sail for the light. "It's a Umeme calling to us," Fred said.

"Full speed for that light!" shouted Captain Eli. "Sadik, could you quickly climb aloft and make sure the flag is unfurled, and bring a lamp with you to shine upon it; we need to let them know that our help is on the way."

"All sails to the wind!" shouted the Chief. "Give it all you've got." The Karu Mar jumped into the waves and was off at full speed."

"Quiz and Blue, get there as soon as possible and let them know our help is coming," shouted Eli

None of the sailors knew exactly what was happening, but they were excited to see the source of that wondrous light, a light that they were headed for at best possible speed.

In little time, the Karu Mar was approaching the light, which was correspondingly dimming and coming lower to the surface of the sea. Quiz spotted the princess floating on the plank, but found no source for the light. Kagayaku was not sure what to make of the rescuers , so she turned off her glow. She was not fully relieved until she recognized the symbols of the Karu Mar lighted on the mast of the approaching ship. She glowed in multiple soft colors, descended, and gently landed on Adalet.

"Awaken, child, we are among the righteous; you will sleep safely on soft clean sheets tonight. Now I am going to disappear for a while; they must not know of my presence. It is best our friendship is not advertised at this time. I will come to you discreetly later tonight."

The ship pulled alongside to rescue Adalet. As she was lifted on board, Captain Eli said "Welcome, child, my ship is at your service."

Sadik stepped forward and welcomed Adalet, saying he would be honored to escort her to her quarters. Rohani bowed her head and welcomed her: "If I may be of any service, please let me know."

Of course, only Grumpy Bill could complain at such a time; he muttered just loud enough for Rohani to hear: "What happened to that wonderful light? Where did it go? Was all of that fuss over this little waif?" he mumbled.

It was not that he was not glad for the rescue, it is just that he thought the light would herald something magnificent. Rohani, who was standing near, deliberately swished her tail to hit him in a delicate area and he winced. To add to the injury, Rohani lightly stepped on his left foot as she walked by. Sadik made note of Rohani's uncharacteristic behavior and took Adalet by the hand to escort her to her quarters.

After they had passed, Rohani asked Eli: "Why is Grumpy Bill even part of the crew, anyway? You heard what he said."

Eli replied: "Everyone has strengths and weaknesses, and sometimes our strengths can be a weakness. Let's take a normally very compassionate donkey for example, oh, here is one right here (as he scratched Rohani behind her ears). You, my dear friend, are quick to believe in the kingdom. You are wonderfully sensitive to others, and most pleasant company, so you assume that those who are not quick to believe, are not pleasant to be around and that appear insensitive, must be somehow falling short of the kingdom."

Eli continued: "While this may be somewhat true, falling short is a problem for every one of us, we just fall short in different areas in our lives. Let me make one thing very clear, all of us are in one way or another undeserving of grace. If we were to assume that we were right in heart only when we were at our best, we could begin to fear that when we were down or discouraged, grace would be far from us. The opposite is more accurate. Grumpy old Bill is here to learn and to exemplify that he is loved and accepted in the kingdom for who he is, not for how wonderfully sociable he is, though he could certainly learn some lessons in that area. The sun shines equally on the just and the unjust, for this is part of the certitude that life is a blessed gift for all."

After Adalet was in bed and fast asleep, Rohani and Sadik commented on how interesting it was that she was completely unperturbed by all the mysteries surrounding her when any normal child would be taken aback.

"I wonder what she knows about the mysteries of life?" Sadik asked.

Captain Eli called an all hands meeting. "You should be aware that the little girl the mysterious light guided us to is the only survivor of a vicious attack that sank her vessel. The others were killed or captured for ransom or to be sold as slaves, and their vessel sunk. Did anybody notice the small design on the border of her shirt? That was the royal crest of a great noble family. She can be none other than the Princess daughter of King Roonaan and Queen Isihe. It is a great mystery that she should have escaped capture, and Prince Toh-kali will be enraged and dangerously dedicated to finding her. With her on board, we are in even more danger than we already were."

"If the evil prince were to have seen the mysterious, disappearing light that called us to rescue her, which is likely, he will be in fast pursuit. Let us hope he now sails in a direction away from, and not towards us. Shall we continue our trip back to the island of the Corbatanos, even if we already know he has spies and allies there? In order to rescue the captives, as we promised, we will be placing ourselves in greatest peril, and she especially will be if she is found, so we must keep her presence secret, for her sake and for ours. So, do we continue our journey to fulfill our word, or do we turn tail and head for home? Never mind, I know your answer – we sail on – but remember the secret."

# Grumpy Bill Shows His True Colors

That very night, the Karu Mar ran into another sudden severe storm at sea. Rohani was on deck with some of the crew while Grumpy Bill was at the helm. Old Bill skillfully kept the ship into the wind and the waves to keep her from being hit broadside. Rohani was helping by keeping tension on one side of a line so that the line could be slowly released to lower one of the sails. Suddenly, a strong gust caught the sail, and one of the securing cleats tore free from the wood. It all happened so fast that Rohani was picked up with the free-flying sail and slung over the side into the stormy waters.

Bill screamed "Rohani is overboard," turned the helm over to another, and, without a second thought, secured a rescue line about himself and dove into the turbulent water to save Rohani. Bill swam, as best he could against the waves and the wind. He could only see Rohani when he was at the crest of a wave; when he went into the trough, he lost sight of her. He had no idea where she was drifting, but he was not going to leave her alone in the storm.

Even in the best of weather, rescuing someone who has gone overboard is a dangerous undertaking that often ends tragically and unsuccessfully. By the time the ship can be re-trimmed for a quick, safe turn a great distance is covered. For Bill to have risked himself in the dark of a storm for the life of a donkey was an amazing feat. Rohani was struggling to keep her head out of the water; she was not even aware that Bill was swimming to her aid.

Back on the ship, the Chief had joined another section of line that was attached to Bill and continued to play out the line for him to continue his search. Neither Bill nor Rohani would be able to swim to the ship in the strong currents. Bill held the lifeline for both to be pulled back on board. As Bill reached the crest of another wave, he observed that he was, amazingly, getting nearer to Rohani. She looked up just in time to see him.

Bill prayed: "I know I have been hard and harsh with this little donkey, please forgive me and let me get her back on board safely."

Simultaneously, Rohani prayed: "I am sorry I judged him wrongly; I was wrong in my heart and in my words. Please keep him safe and let us both get back on board safely."

In but a moment, Blue was by their side and two of his strong arms had wrapped around them. As the crew pulled on the safety line, Blue helped them along and skillfully lifted them back onto the tossing ship, where they were welcomed by all.

After the incident, Grumpy Bill and Rohani were the best of friends, and Bill was even known to sneak a few extra pickled fish to Blue every now and again.

As quickly as it had come, the storm abated. By the next morning, there were favorable winds and the ship sailed smoothly and swiftly. The storm had aided their progress and made up for their lost time. Soon, they were nearing the island of the Corbatanos.

# Clash of Kingdoms

As the Karu Mar approached the harbor on the island of the Corbatanos, they were surprised to see that there was a ship already docked there. But not just any ship. It was the Black Ship of Prince Toh-Kali; easily twice the size of the Karu Mar, and it was bristling with cannons. The black flags she was showing were of a red iron fist and a red dragon.

Unbeknownst to anyone, Adalet had managed to sneak up onto the deck of the Karu Mar to take a look around. One look at the black ship and Adalet turned pale, and she ran trembling below deck. Sadik and Rohani followed, as did Barnabas. As they approached to comfort her, she ran to Barnabas and clung to him.

"There, there, Adalet. We will take care of you, we all promise. What scares you so?

Adalet explained that the ship she saw in the harbor was the very ship that had attacked and

166

sunk the ship on which she was travelling with her parents. "There is evil on board and they will kill us all," she sobbed. Kagayaku tried to calm her, but Adalet was too distraught.

It was then that Rohani heard Fred tell her to take everyone above decks and leave him alone with Adalet. Rohani complied. Once the others were on deck, Fred spoke to Kagayaku, who, heretofore had thought her presence unknown.

'Who speaks?" Adalet asked.

"Who is talking to you, Kagayaku? Is there another Umeme on board?"

"No, there is not." answered Kagayaku. "I would know."

"There is only one other being then, that could speak to you, and even more, to know who you are, my little Umeme friend, Kagayaku. I was there when you were given your name in the pools of Eiennoai. Now, Kagayaku, can you tell your friend that she is most safe under our protection and she need not fear?"

"Adalet, my friend, we have an angel on board with us. I assure you he is more powerful than I am, and I feel safer already, so you can relax, but his presence is to be kept even more secret than mine, so now we are all in secret together."

"I will be here for you, my little glowing friend – oh, and that was a great light show last night," Fred playfully said.

Kagayaku glowed a reddish color and said, "Thanks!"

The Chief asked Eli if the ship should hold off in deeper water, with only a few going forward in the ship's boat to ascertain the situation.

"Good advice, Chief, but we are all in this together. All in favor of taking the ship into the harbor say aye." All but Old Bill did so, and his nay sounded rather hollow in its lonely dissent, but there was one vote missing. Although he would not vote nay, Barnabas was too afraid to vote aye. He just couldn't find his voice.

"Into the thick of it we go," said Eli. "Chief, bring us alongside that ominous floating symbol of evil and we shall see what transpires. Blue and Quiz, you stay hidden so we can use you as a surprise if you are needed."

Just as a show of force to intimidate the Karu Mar, the black ship let loose a broadside of her huge cannons out to sea.

The crew of the Karu Mar was shocked and frightened by the power of the blast.

"Don't worry" said Eli; "The roar of evil is always louder than its actual power. Brave faces, all. Justice and Power are on our side, no matter how much it seems to the contrary. Do not fear, and do not anxiously look about, for we are more protected than you can imagine."

Captain Eli ordered that the Karu Mar be tied to the pier – just on the other side from where Prince Tohkali's ship was tied. The crew of the Karu Mar tried not to show the terror that they were feeling. The black ship had twice the number of cannons and their crew was noticeably larger, stronger, and definitely more experienced in the cruelty of combat. In fact, it seemed they were all too ready to fight just for the 'fun of it.' The evil crew all shook their weapons, clashing them against their shields, and shouted at the Karu Mar in derision:

"Look at the little sissies – oh isn't that cute; look, they have a pet elf-monkey and a donkey, too." Neither Sadik nor Rohani took kindly to the disparagement.

Blue discretely showed his head on the far side of the Karu Mar and whispered, "That is the black ship that fired on me and the dolphins. I told you they were ugly."

Blue just had to get a secret slap in against them, so he swam under their ship undetected and reached up and discreetly shoved one of the sailors into another, which started a fight between them. This infighting, of course, was a common occurrence among the villainous, for such is the character of evil. Their chief had to put a stop to it: "If you want to do some fighting and killing – look over there, not amongst yourselves, you ignorant animals," he shouted.

The diminutive governor came waddling down the pier with an evil smirk on his face. By his side was none other than the evil prince himself, "Prince Toh-Kali."

Captain Eli shouted forth and requested permission to come ashore.

"Permission granted, oh unfortunate one." replied the Governor.

Eli stated, "As per our contractual agreement, we have brought the agreed upon amount of silver to redeem the lives and freedom of the captive Corbatanos."

"The contract is null and void" the Prince coldly said. "This Governor, who shall pay for his insolence, acted beyond his authority in agreeing to free my slaves."

"Well, if that is the case, I hope that you and I could reach another agreement so that they may be freed," Eli stated.

"They shall not be freed, and the price you will pay for interfering in the power of darkness is higher than you realize," the Prince snarled.

"Indeed," said Eli. "And by what higher authority do you make such a declaration? Are you not yourself, but a lowly vassal of the greater evil you serve?"

"Silence, impudent one," Prince Toh-Kali growled. "For that insult the lives of you and your crew are forfeit."

"Ah, yes, but you see, I am also but a servant of another, but this Kingdom is greater than yours and I stand against you in the name of the One True Source of All, whose Kingdom shall be restored."

"Fool, he deserted this place long ago and only children and grandmother Lusans still believe in the promise of that kingdom. The power of

171

Darkness rules now; not your fairy tale 'Once Upon a Time' kingdom."

Captain Eli responded. "Then I propose a test to see which power is indeed greater. To the victor belong all the spoils, and the loser shall serve the winner. What do you say? Do you not want a chance to prove your bravado, or are you afraid of the challenge of combat?"

Prince Toh-Kali shook with an evil laughter that echoed coldly from his throat. It seemed the air grew colder, and all but Eli shook with fear.

"Fool, I accept your challenge. I was going to just murder you all outright and steal your ship and your treasures, but a clash of kingdoms is even better. You chose the combat, I will even let you set the terms. Go ahead and make the last executive decision you shall ever make; I am intrigued."

"Well and good," stated Captain Eli. "I choose trial by mortal combat; me against you, or if you are afraid to meet me, you may choose another champion. Choose your best, and I defy you."

"I accept, foolish little captain. The combat will take place over there on that beach where both crews can watch the outcome. Crew of the Karu Mar, prepare your death rituals, for you are soon to die. Pray to your fairy tale King of Kindness, then standby and witness the power of the Darkness. Captain Eli, go to the beach and await my champion."

"So, you are not going to fight me yourself, you are going to send someone else? No interference, then, me against your champion and that is all. Do we agree?"

"Oh, yes, yes, yes. My champion is undefeated in battle against Lusan and beast and needs no assistance. As for your pitiful crew, it wouldn't do you any good if they all joined you in combat, for they would all die with you, but I want my crew to have some fun in combat killing your pitiful bunch after you have fallen. And fall you shall."

Hearing this permission for battle, the crew of the Black Ship shrieked and screamed with delight and banged their swords and hurled more insults and cursing at the crew of the Karu Mar.

Captain Eli confidently walked down the pier and over to the beach. He knelt down in the sand and prepared his heart for battle. "Forbid it, my King, that I should fight in anger or revenge, for You alone are worthy to Judge in the affairs of life. Guide me, I pray, to fight in Your strength and for Your Justice alone."

Prince Toh-Kali, armed with a huge long bow and a quiver of fire arrows followed, but it was not he who was going to meet Eli in battle. He stood and observed. The evil prince waved his hand and a horrid trumpet blast rang out from the deck of the Black Ship. All on board the Karu Mar looked around, wondering what the trumpet call was all about. Soon, off in the distance, a great dragon could be seen flying towards them.

"Behold my champion" shrieked the Prince. "You fool, prepare to die."

As the dragon approached and landed on the beach in front of Eli, all could see that it was almost equal in size to the King of Dragons, but this one was bright red, with cold black eyes. Its scales were jagged, and its body was more heavily armored. Upon seeing that Eli's adversary in a fight to the death was such an undefeatable foe, the crew of the Karu Mar despaired as the crew of the black ship cheered and jeered. Prince Toh-Kali spoke to the dragon in its evil, guttural language and said: "Do not kill him too quickly, oh evil one; let us have some entertainment for my crew."

The dragon spoke to Eli, "Prince Toh-Kali wants me to have some fun with you before I kill you, so let us dance, shall we?"

174

"Well and good, old Malpirius, betrayer of the two Kings. Judgment comes to you this day. The time of the old Kingdom is restored. This day I will take from you your treasures." (This is one of the greatest insults any could give to a dragon, for his pride was in the treasures he possessed.)

"Fairy tales, little one, it was I and my followers who defeated the King of Dragons long ago and your kingdom is lost and gone, for there is no remedy against the power of the Evil Lord."

"We shall see. I give you first strike, old lizard," said Eli. "Make your move."

Malpirius let out a roar of anger and swung his mighty tail around to catch Eli, but he was too fast. Eli used his spear to vault over the tail. He rolled to the side and under the great beast and then thrust it between the scales of the underside of the dragon.

"Tricky move, little one. I actually felt that little tickle, but your spear cannot produce a wound of any consequence against me. I am the harbinger of death and destruction."

"Really." answered Eli. Perhaps you should carry less thunder in your mouth and more lightning. Do you not have eyes and a throat that would

175

not fare well with a stab? How would you like to go through life as a blinded worm?"

"Try to catch my eye, little one, and I shall devour you in one bite." With that the dragon lunged toward the captain with his mouth opened wide. Eli, expecting the move, thrust his spear into the tongue of the great beast, driving the shaft in deep, then he rolled to the side.

The dragon let out a great roar of pain. He was shocked, for he had not felt any wound for centuries. He shook his head violently and finally dislodged the spear as blood spurted from the wound. "Can I roast him now?" the dragon asked Prince Toh-Kali.

"Sure, let him have it." answered the Prince. "My crew is spoiling for the kill."

The great dragon let loose a gigantic plume of raging fire that completely enveloped Captain Eli. The crew of the Black Ship roared with delight, and the crew of the Karu Mar fell to their knees. When the flame subsided, there stood Captain Eli, unscathed. The look on the dragon's face changed from one of smug victory to total shock. Again, the dragon blasted and again Eli withstood.

"Who are you?" asked the dragon in unbelief. "How is this possible? I have flamed and none have survived. I have even burned dragons. How can this be?"

"It is as I have said," Eli responded. "The old Kingdom is restored. I was given a little gift from the King of Dragons, who once again wears the great fire ruby around his noble neck. Captain Eli pulled back his sleeve and revealed the Kohatu Wakawa, from which a blinding light shone forth. "Bow, Malpirius. My judgment is that both your sight and your fire are now taken from you. Listen to my terms, for they can set you free."

"Immediately blinded and without flame, Malpirius muttered: "You have the Kohatu Wakawa – how is this possible?"

"I told you, it is a gift from the King of Dragons who would call you back into the service of good. Do you agree to terms of surrender, or shall we continue this battle with you so vulnerable? Even if you should win (which is highly unlikely) then you will go through life blind and flameless; vulnerable to attacks from your many enemies, and, of course, unable to appreciate the beauty of all of your treasures. Your eyes will turn the pale greyish-blue color of death and all will mock you.

"Yes, yes, I surrender; I cannot argue" said the defeated dragon. The thought of being flameless

177

and blind and at the mercy of others was too much for the beast.

"I recognize the stone and its power, which defeats me, but I thought it was lost forever. This cannot be happening. This could only mean that you are the chosen one who is to prepare the way of the King. Over time, I lost faith and I thought the prophecies were just myth and fairy tales; I yield. Blind and with no power of fire, I cannot prevail. The judgment is too much for me; I surrender. What is my task, and I shall fulfill it."

"Because you have humbled your soul and surrendered, you shall have your sight restored, even now." He pointed the stone toward the dragon and a gentle light fell upon the dragon's eyes, restoring his sight.

Upon seeing that the dragon had surrendered and planned to aid in the restoration of the Old Kingdom, Prince Toh-Kali could not contain his rage. He drew his bow, and sent forth two flaming arrows towards Eli, who was only a short distance away. Within the twinkling of an eye, there was another flash of light, but this one shot forth from the hold of the Karu Mar. The light formed a glowing shield and blocked the path of the arrows. As all watched, the light took full form, and there stood Fred, all eleven feet of him; an angel in full shining glory.

"Thanks, Fred," said Eli.

"Don't mention it, Eli." responded the angel.

"Way to go, Fred!" Rohani shouted from the deck of the ship.

# Prince Toh-Kali Humiliated

Fred then approached the terrified Prince Toh-Kali, grabbed him and lifted him up in the air by the throat as Eli, Malpirius and the two ship's crews watched the encounter.

"I was waiting for your treachery, slimy one" said Fred. Still, forgiveness is offered to you this day; if you will surrender your hatred and repent of your evil, you will be freed."

"Me, surrender, never!" shouted Toh-Kali. This battle is over, but we shall win the war. Your days are numbered, and I will dance on your dead body."

"Angels know no death, you sad, clueless, and repugnant being. Forgiveness was offered to two beings today. The dragon was wise enough to accept, and he shall be blessed. You, however, have proven once again one of the mysteries of evil.

Some say the fact that you exist proves that love does not exist, but here we are together. One's freedom to choose between good and evil, unfortunately, results in your existence, but you always were, always have been, and always shall be the loser. Come on, loser, I will return you to your ship."

The crew of the Karu Mar watched as Fred then flew the still dangling, hapless Prince, who was powerless in Fred's grip, over to his ship and dropped him on the deck from a good height, causing him to land a most awkward and unceremonious landing. The angel drew a flaming sword and pointed it at the trembling crew.

"Your champions are defeated. Continue to follow this evil one if you want to, but I suggest a different path, for judgment is coming against all the wicked. Choose a new life for yourselves and be free. Who here is weary of this heartless evil and wishes to come with me and be free?" The Lusans looked around, but none had the courage to accept the offer.

"This is another problem with this world," Fred said. "Lusans are afraid to stand up against evil, even if it means they are thereby choosing to remain tormented by it."

From the back of the group, only one stepped forward. Although he was threatened and taunted by the crew with insults that do not bear repeating, he boldly stated; "I will take that offer; if you will take me with you, I will go."

Fred responded: "A lost one restored. I have to tell you that my friends are dancing right now, for this is a joyous event; let us get out of here." That said, Fred grabbed him by the arm and immediately flew him over to the deck of the Karu Mar and addressed the crew:

"This one wants to know how to live for the kingdom; teach him well. You will not see me again unless I choose it to be so. Prepare for battle, if needed; Captain Eli will want to get back to the mission of rescuing the Corbatanos."

Fred winked at Rohani, and then, POOF, he disappeared.

Back on the black ship, Prince Toh-Kali was furious. He was enraged over his humiliating defeat and embarrassed by being unceremoniously dropped onto the deck of his ship in front of his crew. Predictably, he took his anger out on them. The crew of the Karu Mar watched as he began to bark orders for them to prepare to sail immediately. He pulled out his sword and threatened to kill anyone who hesitated to obey, or who even thought of deserting the ship.

"Desertion will be punished by slow death. That angel thing may be powerful, but there is a power of evil that is greater than he, and I will make that angel pay, make no mistake about it. Now, get us out to sea, we sail back to the castle. I shall have my revenge. Eli and that shiny fellow shall pay with their lives for my insult." Within minutes, the black ship was out to sea, with many on the crew wondering why they did not take Fred's offer.

# Redemption

Eli returned his attention to Malpirius: "For all of us there is a chance for redemption. Here are the terms: You are to return every bit of stolen treasure that you are able to restore, but do not despair. Choose to restore the injury, and you may still keep all of the remaining treasures when you cannot find the rightful owners, or if the return of the treasure would finance any injustice. Still, I assure you, you will find keeping your treasures will not bring you as much joy as you find in giving them away. The King of Dragons sends his greetings and asks that you take your rightful place in defending justice, and not in perverting it as you have done. He will welcome you if you will return to the ancient ways. Go and fulfill your vow and you shall be free."

"And can it be that I should again fly with the King of Dragons after my treachery? Do you think he will forgive me?" asked the dragon.

"Ask him yourself when you see him," said Eli. "You shall find him, or he shall find you before long. I have a feeling you still have a part to play in the restoration of the kingdom. Oh, and there is one more small task for you to perform as part of your healing of hatred between Lusan and dragons. Do you know of an island that had a name change to Cockroach Island? There is a plant that grows there, a small spice plant that can provide healing.

"Yes, all dragons know of this place, it was once called Spice Island, but we call it Mashal's island. It is Yamba Kusamvana, the birthplace of the war."

Eli responded: "The birthplace of war is soon to be the place of healing; the treasure I ask you to bring is a healing flower that grows at the side of Mashal's grave.

Malpirius was shocked to the core. "First, how do you know of Mashal's grave? And, secondly, it is not possible that anything should grow anywhere near Mashal's grave, for it was sealed with the dragon fire of a hundred vengeful dragons. The heat of this would destroy all life on it forever. Even the soil would die, and you say a flower of healing grows therefrom?"

"You, my friend, should know of the power of sacrificial love. You know how Mashal knowingly flew into a trap to willingly give his life to save a younger dragon from death. As he lay dying, Mashal wept not only for the injury to the dragons, but for the bigger tragedy of the brokenness of the harmony that once existed among Lusans and dragons and all life.

As Mashal's tears mingled with his blood, all heaven took notice. It is no surprise, then, that at the right time, the blood and tears he shed would restore life and allow for this healing flower, a Malekia, to grow from his grave. For all-too-many dragons, Mashal's death became a justification for the Great War against all Lusans. Sadly, the war also divided the dragons between those would not condemn all Lusans, the innocent along with the guilty, and those who would."

Eli continued: "The King of Dragons remained faithful to mercy, even though it cost him the unity of his kingdom, and the greatest of sorrows. Your vengefulness, Malpirius, caused you to turn against the innocent along with the guilty, against your own kind, and against your King. But I have come to announce that now is the time of redemption, now is the time of restoration, and all shall be healed, but sadly, not without further conflict.

"Please, go to Mashal's island. Carefully take but one flower, leaving the rest to grow in secret, and bring it with you to a small island some 40 miles south southwest from here. There, you will find a single solitary Lusan marooned on that island. He holds an immense hatred for all dragons, and he will likely curse your arrival and hurl any number of insults at you. Whatever he says, do not let it anger you. Although it would seem he deserves it, do not blast him and turn him into a crispy critter."

The Red Dragon laughed to himself and repeated "Crispy critter?"

"He is mostly blind, but he will sense you are near. Let him know I have sent you and that you are there to help him. If he lets go of his hatred, lower your head and offer to fly him to his home to provide healing for his granddaughter. One more important thing, he must never know the origin of the flower's power. It must have no connection to dragons – not because of his hatred, for this shall pass, but because the future requires this secret. Not even your fellow dragons must know of this power.

Oh, and I ask one more little favor; once he is riding along with you, please buzz by and circle my ship once so he can wave at us. I want to see his face, and my crew needs to know that you are the help that I said was to come to him. Thank, you, my-once-enemy, and now my friend. Go in peace."

"I will go to fulfill my vows" said the dragon. "I hope we meet again, Captain Eli." The dragon bowed his head and then he lifted his wings in flight. As he flew over the rapidly fleeing Black Ship of Prince Toh-Kali, Malpirius let loose the most powerful blast of fire that any had ever seen. He circled the ship with a great ring of fire, then specifically targeted his image on the ship's flag, and burned it to a crisp. Malpirius then flew off to find the healing flower and then to find the marooned Captain Horace.

# Malpirius and Captain Horace

As he continued marooned on that small island, what Horace did not know was that the only hope to save his precious Melissa could only come from the dragons that he hated so much. Most ironically, what he would never be allowed to know, was the healing flower that he sought had bloomed from the sacrificial blood of a dragon. The fact that Mashal's blood was that powerful was one of the deepest secrets that only a chosen few were to be allowed to know.

Captain Horace was fuming mad over his predicament. Already five days had passed marooned on the small island which held no food or water sources, and he had only two week's provisions. What kind of a monster was Eli to trick him like that? He could have at least given him the opportunity to try and find the Cockroach Island and rescue his granddaughter. But no, he marooned him.

"There must be a deeper reason behind what Eli is doing." Horace thought to himself. "Now, what was that last question he asked me? Oh yeah, which was greater: hatred or love?"

Right now, his hatred for Eli almost equaled that of his hatred for dragons; it seemed hatred was winning. But then he thought of his granddaughter and the love and the trust and the laughter in her eyes. He must not fail her. Something in his heart made him realize this was a test of his soul, and, at the top of his voice Horace screamed "Please, help me save my precious Melissa. Love is greater than hate and I surrender, just give me a chance to love. I would forgive and hug and kiss a dragon if that would get me off this island and let me share with my Melissa."

As soon as he said this, Horace heard the sound of giant wings swooping closely over him. Coming in for a landing right before him was the very same Red Dragon that had, in the past, taken one of his ships, cost him many of his crew, and even one of his legs many years before. Though nearly blind, he could see the enormous size of the dragon, hear its breathing, and even feel the heat of each breath. Forgetting the confession he had just made, the memories from sensing the Red Dragon overwhelmed him and he shouted out in anger:

"Have you now come to taunt me in my despair, evil lizard?"

The great dragon spoke: "It is not a good nor a wise act to curse a dragon that stands before you, angry little one, besides, I have a gift for you. I was sent by Captain Eli to bring you this flower for your loved one. Malpirius reached forth one of his great claws, in which the healing flower was carefully hidden. As he smelled the beautiful fragrance that emanated from the flower, Horace could not believe what was happening.

The dragon bowed his great head, laying it onto the sand: "Come, fly with me for the need is great and the hourglass is near its end for your granddaughter."

"Great dragon, do you mean that you understand my needs and you will take me and the flower to save my precious Melissa?"

Malpirius spoke: "Yes to all your questions. There is no time to argue. Trust me now, or it will be too late. Lay aside your hatred and let us fly together."

"Hatred has no place if it interferes with love. Help me save my Melissa and we shall be friends for life."

"Let it be so; climb up, friend. Here, you keep the flower safe in your pocket and hold on tight with both hands; our flight must be swift."

Horace located the flower by sensing its beautiful smell; he kissed and guarded the precious treasure. As fast as he could, he climbed on to the dragon and they were soon airborne, flying at incredible speed. In but a moment's time, Malpirius had spotted the Karu Mar and was, as directed by Eli, conducting a fly by.

Malpirius said: "Captain Horace, I am going to pass by the Karu Mar, so turn your head to the left and wave at your friends."

As they flew low, alongside the Karu Mar, the ship's crew was shocked to see Horace, the known hater of dragons, now riding on the back of the Red Dragon and waving happily at them. There was a smile of amusement and peace on the face of Horace as he passed by the ship, and Captain Eli rejoiced in the healing he knew was already happening. He turned to his crew and spoke:

"Never underestimate the power of grace. The dragon is flying Horace and a healing flower back so that Melissa can be healed."

By evening that day, the dragon had covered three months' time at sea and Horace could sense they were approaching his island. As they flew near, alarm bells were sounded and all the people panicked, running for cover as they saw that the giant beast was going to land right in their plaza. They were all convinced their doom was certain. One of the guards in an observation tower shouted out: "I see a person riding upon the back of the dragon." As the dragon approached, Horace called out to the terrified people to assure them there was no need for fear.

"It is I, Captain Horace," he shouted. "The dragon comes in peace, and he brought me here so that Melissa could be healed."

To the amazement of the villagers, the dragon landed softly in their plaza. Horace dismounted the dragon and, for a blind Lusan with only one leg, made it up the hill to Melissa's house with amazing speed.

The dragon, which was too large to pass through the narrow streets, circled around to the back of the property so he could be there for Melissa's healing. The still terrified villagers followed the dragon at a distance, wondering what was going to happen next.

The doctor was there with Melissa; he had a grim look on his face. He had already stated, "She is no longer with us." and Dorothy was distraught with tears. Horace entered the room and cried out, "Precious child, I am here with your healing."

Little Melissa appeared lifeless, but after all he had seen and the change in his heart, Horace knew that it was as sure as the sunshine that she would be healed. He took the plant and broke open the flower under Melissa's nose. The entire room was suddenly filled with the most wonderful aroma; it was the smell of a pine forest after a rain, gardenias in bloom, of jasmine, and sugar, and cinnamon all rolled into one. If heaven had an incense, this was it.

When Melissa stirred, she smiled a weak but precious smile. Horace ground up the petals of the flower into some water for her to drink, and as Melissa drank it up, all her color was literally restored right before their eyes. Melissa opened her eyes and said, "Oh, grandfather, I knew you would come, I just knew it. I dreamed of Captain Eli and the Chimono and magic islands and wonderful dragons, and suddenly you are here."

"Dragons did you say? Wonderful dragons? Would you like to see a wonderful dragon right now? Then let me just carry you over to the window." Horace suddenly scooped her up in his arms, ignoring the protests of her aunt and the doctor, and opened the window to show her the dragon.

"Hello, Melissa," said the dragon. "I hope you continue to get healthier every day. When you are ready, I promise to take you for a ride over the mountains and over the ocean."

"You mean, I could actually fly on a dragon?" she asked. "Oh, I will get well, now I must get well, in fact I am feeling 'weller' and 'weller' right now. Thank you, grandfather, and thank you, Great Dragon, you look like a very nice dragon."

The kind and innocent words of the child penetrated into the dragon's heart like a knife; the words were like healing to the soul of the old dragon and he wondered how he could have ever denied himself the treasure of love while seeking revenge or greedily destroying others for their treasures of gold and silver. Tears of joy and remorse flowed from his eyes and he bowed to Melissa. This also penetrated the heart of Horace and he wondered how he could have allowed hatred to poison his soul to the degree that he could not see the goodness before him and around him. And see it he could, for contact with the flower had perfectly healed the captain's eyes, and he lived to see his young grand daughter grow into a beautiful young Lusan.

"Thank you, child," the dragon, I shall try to live up to those words."

Horace spoke from the window: "You already have, my one-time-enemy-now-my-friend." And with that, he bowed to the dragon and the dragon returned the sign. Then, in a customary dragon fashion, sealed the friendship by roaring forth a great blast of fire into the air. The dragon burned his mark into a boulder in the yard, warning all other dragons this place was under his protection.

"I am off, but I shall return to take you and Melissa on a flight, you have my word." The dragon flew off and was out of sight in but a moment's time.

# Justice is Served

All the crew members were talking excitedly about the way the Red Dragon was now in league with Eli and how Fred had appeared out of nowhere to save Captain Eli. The Chief of the Boat commented: "I was right here when I heard a woosh and saw a burst of light. That angel must have been on board the ship; It looked like he flew straight out of a cannon port. Has he been with us all along? How was it that nobody has never seen him before?"

Blue added that he was sure the angel came out of the ship: "I was in the water right beside the ship and he flew right over me," he said.

Sadik jumped in and said: "I think someone has been holding out on us. I think there is someone who knew of the angel. I won't mention any names, but her initials are R.O.H.A.N.I. Am I right, Miss Donkey?"

"Now, how is it that the entire crew has been in and out of the hold hundreds of times and never seen him, yet you think that I have?" she asked.

"Well, I still think you knew about this all along," Sadik said.

While they all were absorbed in discussing the events, Eli had quietly returned to the Karu Mar and addressed the crew: "You are all very privileged to have seen my friend and guardian angel, Fred, but you must be careful with this knowledge. Angels are not meant to be commonly seen or heard; they want to do their duty without people even thinking about them, and especially without people seeking after them. They are beings more powerful than you could ever imagine, but they are messengers, protectors, and servants, not beings to be worshipped. We all should act like angels to seek justice and fight to protect the innocent. When danger arises, do not expect an angel to defend you, one may or may not be there; your fate is up to a higher power than them. Of course, you can be amazed by all of this, but from day to day, just live your life and do your duty and leave the seeking of angels alone."

"You are correct, Sadik. Rohani did know of my friend Fred. Notice how she never mentioned her ability to see and talk to Fred. Emulate her behavior."

"For now, though, we have more pressing matters to attend to. The Governor's soldiers are still keeping those poor captives in chains in the mines. One would think that after seeing the ignominious defeat of their Prince, they would wise up. Did I not warn them I would demand justice? I am going to try one more time to see if I can convince them to surrender their captives and offer them to surrender themselves to be allowed to leave peacefully. If they refuse, then we will have to take them by force. Prepare for battle, but it will not be a frontal assault. They are so afraid of Prince Toh-Kali that they will do anything to keep his orders. Some, but not all, are so warped that they would sooner kill their captives than allow them to be freed."

"If anyone approaches the ship intending to surrender, they are to be treated well. Guard them carefully against any treachery, but they are not to be imprisoned. Blue, if anyone does surrender and come on board, let them know you are here so they can see there is no escaping your long arms of justice, so to speak," he said with a smile.

"Quiz, let them know they will be very well roasted if they try anything. I want you all to stay on board. If I do not return within the hour, you will know that my attempt at peace has failed and you must take any action you think necessary to free the captives. Chief, you have the command "

Eli left the ship and headed for the tent of the Governor. Two guards, who had witnessed how the encounter with the dreaded Red Dragon ended in the captain's favor, cautiously approached him and warned him that the Governor gave orders for him to be killed upon sight.

Eli responded: "Thank you for the warning. I understand you are just following orders, but I suggest you step aside. It would be better for you to go down to my ship now and surrender yourselves to my crew. You will be under my protection, and no harm or punishment will come to you. This is your opportunity for freedom from the tyranny of Prince Toh-Kali. Three of his crew are already safely on my ship – not in irons, mind you – but free of the tyranny of evil because they chose to surrender. Remember, your Evil Prince was picked up by the throat and dropped onto his ship, and he quickly sailed away in defeat. You may choose to fight for him, but you will only suffer loss and imprisonment. The choice is yours, distinguished soldiers. I am going to speak with that confused and contrary Lusan falsely titled the

Governor of this island." Eli pulled his sword from its scabbard and stated: "What is it gonna be, fight or freedom? It is decision time."

They looked at each other and came to the same conclusion. "We prefer the chance for freedom," they said.

"Good choice," said Eli; he sheathed his sword and then he walked straight into the governor's tent. "I am here to offer you amnesty for all your crimes if you surrender yourself and your soldiers and release the captives."

The Governor responded with rage. "How did you get past my guards?"

Eli replied, "Oh, do you mean the guards that were wise enough to surrender to me and are now walking to my ship to surrender themselves? You mean those guards? Hopefully, you will be as wise as they are and accept my terms."

"They will pay for their betrayal!" the Governor screamed.

"Do you really think so?" asked Eli. "There are two things you apparently have not realized: one, we could have imprisoned or killed Prince Toh-Kali earlier, and two, he is not here to protect you. You are powerless either way, so please save yourself and me the trouble of any violence. Do the right thing, surrender and let the Corbatanos have their freedom."

"Never!" shouted the Governor.

Eli responded: "How sad that your heart is so cold, be it from fear or from selfishness. Even so, you have chosen your fate. This is not over."

"Captain Eli," the mayor said deridingly, "If you try anything at all, I will have those captives all killed. You have been warned."

Eli responded: "And I will ensure punishment is given for every ounce of injury inflicted upon them. Now you have been warned."

Eli left the tent, headed towards the barracks of the soldiers, and walked straight in.

"If I may have your attention, I am here to offer you amnesty if you surrender and agree to release the captives. I give you my word of honor that you will not be imprisoned, and you will all be treated well. I promise you freedom here, or safe passage to the next inhabited island where you will be given a new opportunity for freedom and a new life. Your defeated Prince has deserted you and that crazy fool falsely called the Governor plans to order you to fight against me and my crew. If you fight, you will lose, I can assure you, and then those that survive will be imprisoned. Who among you is wise enough to come with me now?"

The Sergeant of the Guard, a terrifying figure pushed his way forward and mockingly said: "You should not have come in here alone, you foolish seafarer." He turned to the soldiers and ordered them to seize Eli.

Eli countered: "Soldiers, this is your last chance, come with me now and you will be spared." With that, Eli turned towards the door, but the Sergeant moved to stand in the way.

Eli stated: "Sergeant, since you are unyielding, I challenge you to a sword duel; a fight to the death, if you will. You against me, unless you are afraid. I promise that my friend, who carried off Prince Toh-Kali, will not interfere with our duel. It will be just me and you, and the winner decides the fate of the Corbatanos and your soldiers. What do you say, Sergeant? Are you brave enough to accept the challenge?"

The Sergeant answered: "I already have the advantage; I can kill you or take you prisoner now, why should I accept your challenge?"

Eli replied: "Because it is a matter of pride and honor. If you refuse a challenge now, your soldiers will count it as cowardice and you will forever be branded as one who refused to accept a duel, you low-life person of questionable lineage, that is why." As the soldiers mumbled amongst themselves in agreement, the Sergeant knew that he would have to accept the challenge.

Eli chided the Sergeant: "So, get your sword and step outside. Your soldiers can watch how well you handle yourself against some random sea captain."

The Sergeant of the Guard did not want to accept the challenge, but pride and protocol demanded that he did. He would have preferred to just have his soldiers swarm Captain Eli and be done with him. However, he was convinced he could easily take Eli in a duel anyway, so he stepped out to meet him in mortal combat.

Eli asked: "Do you have any terms, any rules you would like to set for our duel, or is it just survivor takes all?"

The guard responded: "Just draw your sword and prepare to die. Let's get on with this. Before you die, remember, it was your foolish mistake to challenge a superior warrior."

Eli returned: "And remember, it was your foolish mistake to not accept my gracious terms for a peaceful surrender."

The battle did not last long. Eli prevailed throughout the conflict; dodging and parrying every move from the Sergeant. Eli's adversary was so exhausted and desperate to win, that, in his rage, he telegraphed his moves. Eli caught the Sergeant off guard, dodged the attack, slid in behind him and drove the flat of his sword hilt down hard on the back of his head; the adversary crumpled to the ground unconscious. Eli turned his back and slowly walked towards the soldiers.

"My offer of amnesty still stands. Stay here with your fallen leader if you want, or come with me." Several soldiers decided to follow him to freedom.

Eli had deliberately only knocked the Sergeant unconscious rather than killing him. The Sergeant woke up in time to see that he had been unconscious on the ground, so he knew he could have been easily killed. As his eyes came into focus, he saw Eli and some of his soldiers leaving. "Wait," the Sergeant called out. "Why did you spare my life when you know full well I would not have spared yours? If you will wait for me to get my legs under me, I would be honored to serve with you if you would accept my sword."

205

Eli responded, "Did a simple blow on the head knock that much sense into you? Have you really changed, are you willing to do what is right?"

"My whole life has been dedicated to a sense of duty. I did not agree with my masters, but I was duty-bound to comply. Now, I offer you the same dedication of duty, but for the first time in my life, I serve because my heart is indebted. Thanks for sparing my life, Captain."

"A life worth saving, evidently," Eli said. "Come along, Sergeant, the adventure continues."

The crew of the Karu Mar saw the group of them coming at a distance and noticed that Eli was walking in front of the Sergeant of the Guard and six soldiers. At first, the crew was not sure if Eli was a prisoner, and old Bill mumbled that Eli had gone and got himself captured, but then they noticed he still had his sword and he was talking freely with them all. When they arrived on the ship, Eli instructed the crew to welcome them as guests, and gave orders for them to pull out of the harbor.

"We will make it appear as if we are abandoning the quest to rescue the Corbatanos."

Eli turned to the Sergeant and said "I am concerned that the guards over the mines may drop grenades on the miners to kill them if we were to try a rescue, do you think they actually would?"

"I am afraid that they would do just that. I think it would be best to wait until this evening when those poor captives are let out of the mines for the day and then we will not have to worry about anyone dropping grenades down into the shafts during a rescue attempt. Because they will think we have withdrawn, we can lie in wait and take out the guards by surprise.

"Good idea" said Eli. "Quiz, when we begin the engagement, your mission is to fly over the guards to distract them from using their grenades; and yes, you may use a little fire to persuade them, if necessary."

"With pleasure," Quiz said with a smile.

# The Black Ship Revisited

By this time, the black ship was far out to sea and Prince Toh-Kali continued his verbal abuse of his crew. Suddenly, Fred appeared again on their ship and stood silently behind the Prince, who did not see him. Toh-Kali had raised his sword to threaten the crew just as Fred appeared behind him. The crew all dropped back in fear – not of the prince's sword, but of Fred, but Toh-Kali thought he was the one who had inspired their fear. At that point, Fred tapped him on the shoulder. When the Prince turned around, he screamed a high-pitched girly scream and dropped his sword in fear as Fred raised his own sword, which was engulfed in flames.

"I'll be watching you, Evil Prince" he said with a smile. "I will be watching you all. Now that you have had a chance to think about it, does anybody else want to change his ways and choose a life of freedom?"

Two soldiers stepped forward and said "We, also, would like to surrender, if you will forgive us and take us with you." Toh-Kali threatened them with death, but they approached Fred, anyway.

Fred responded: "It is not in my power to forgive, but it is in my power to protect those who call, and to help you seek to do right. Oh, and by the way, ignoble Prince, the crew of the Karu Mar are already calling you Prince Toh-Cuckoo instead. I will be watching you. See ya," Fred took each one by the arm and they disappeared in a flash.

Fred took the two and suddenly appeared on the Karu Mar. "Here are two more who are to be treated kindly and given the chance to follow the path of justice.

# From Chains to Riches

The battle to free the enslaved Corbatanos turned out to be completed without incident. Fortunately, the ruse of withdrawal caused the guards to relax their vigil and then the Sergeant of the Guard convinced all the soldiers that if they would comply with Captain Eli's commands, they would all be granted their freedom. Some of the Corbatanos had wanted to hang the governor and the few soldiers that had refused to surrender, and threatened to beat them and hang them, but Eli rebuked them and assured them justice would be given. Eli then marched the now captive captors, past the free and taunting crowd and placed them in the island prison.

Along with chief Arasibo, Eli called an assembly of all the people:

"Before you condemn all of these soldiers, you should understand their situation. Most of them did not willingly choose to align themselves with

Toh-Kali. One of the evil tactics Toh-Kali employs is to conquer a village or town in order to recruit more forces. Those unwilling to join are subjected to a horrible choice: to either have their family tortured and killed while they are forced to watch, or to join. All it takes is the slaying of one, sister, mother, wife or child and the choice to join becomes easy. How would you choose?"

Eli reminded them that, as they had once been enslaved, they should be yet more merciful people and to never enslave others, but to always deliver those in bonds.

The chief agreed and said "Let us be done with the ugliness of hatred; it is time to celebrate." He turned to his people and said: "You are Corbatanos, so I know you have not forgotten how to celebrate as in the days of old, so let us eat and drink and dance and sing to celebrate our freedom! Your former guards among you here shall not be mistreated. They were under the thumb of evil and they risked their own lives by disobeying the orders to kill you all rather than allow you to be rescued. If you cannot yet accept them, at least do not seek their harm, for this would make you just as guilty as they were."

The Corbatanos, joined by the ship's cook had been preparing a great feast for the freed prisoners all day. They were warned to not drink or eat too much after all the times of deprivation because it would prove too much for their systems, so the feast was composed of many small servings of all the delicious foods they had been deprived of so they could still celebrate.

Eli spoke to the crowd: "Tomorrow, those who have families that have not yet come here to join you can go back to your families, but you will not go back empty handed; you will all go back as very wealthy Corbatanos. The crew of the Karu Mar has agreed to turn over to you the ransom money that would have gone to the Governor and Prince Toh-Cukoo. All the wages that you were deprived of, all of the produce of these mines, will be compensated back to you so that you will be wealthier than the ones who abused you. The Visala gave us 50 million dollars in silver to redeem you. Your old friends gave it all to us in silver out of their love for you. As your captors refused to accept it, it is now yours. Because of your years of slavery, when someone asks how you got your wealth, you can truthfully say you dug it from the earth with your own hands.

The chief tells me there are forty seven of you; this means that you are all millionaires. 2 million will go to support the widows and families of your land who were killed in the mines. Use your money wisely as a blessing to others and you will be rich beyond your riches. 1 million is left for the good of all. Build churches and bridges and schools and take care of the poor among you."

"The Visala send their greetings and offer to trade with you once again. They are a most proud and wonderful people with some strange sense of humor, but they are honorable."

Eli then gave an inside joke: "Even Blue likes them, if you can imagine that, although he says they taste funny." Blue and the crew all laughed, but the Corbatanos did not get the joke. "Anyway, celebrate, rest well, and live free. The time of the restoration of the Old Kingdom is at hand."

The celebrations continued long into the night with much rejoicing that the nightmare of captivity was finally over. Eli gave instructions to the COB to not awaken the crew the next morning, but to let them sleep off their party time. Old Bill and Panday had agreed to stand the the worst night watches into the early morning hours before sunrise so the younger crew could celebrate later into the night and then sleep in.

The Corbatanos were most grateful for their rescue; they were amazed that the crew would go to such great lengths and to even risk their lives to rescue complete strangers, and they honored them all.

# Homeward Bound

L ate in the morning, once the mayor and the prisoners had been locked in the ship's prison, the crew of the Karu Mar was finally assembled on board. Eli addressed them all:

"Chapter one of our great journey is almost over. You have done well and have accomplished much. We are heading back to your homes now. You can decide on the journey home, or after some time at home, whether you wish to go on with chapter two or not. Celebrate your lives with family and friends. When the time comes for a call to stay or continue your adventures; you can make your final decision at that time. Chief, secure the ship for departure, we are heading home, with only one more surprise in store."

After they were underway, Panday approached Eli and said:

"I know rhymes grate on your nerves, so I will give you one of my own, just so it sticks in your head and you answer me:

*"It has been an adventure, this much is sure,*
*but how much more must I endure?*
*My heart is still broken by the loss of my son,*
*for just one more blessing, could I be the one?"*

Eli responded, *"Panday, you deserve blessings, this much is true, but I don't want to spoil the surprise for you."* and then he walked away with a smile.

Along their journey home, Quiz approached Eli one evening with a request, "Captain Eli, is the island of the golden people near our route to the home of the others?"

"We could easily make it so, with little loss of time, why do you ask?"

"Well, I was just thinking; it is not that I do not feel loved and accepted by you all, it is just that the Doradorans told me I was family and I think that there is something more I am supposed to do for them. I have no idea what it is, but I think I should go back there for a while. If you ever need me, or just want to drop in and say 'howdy!' I will be there."

Eli responded: "It is most important that you should follow your heart. I know of many people who have caused themselves and others great sorrow by neglecting to do so. I will inform you when we are near. Do you wish a big send-off, or do you want to sneak away without a good-bye?"

"I don't think I would do too well with good-byes," responded Quiz. "Please just thank the crew. Tell them I love them all, and that I received a request from the Doradorans that I just had to answer."

"As you wish," responded Eli. "We will all miss you very much. Take care, my little Quizzenrofflesnozinbloken."

"Just Quiz will do," Quiz said with a smile.

One morning, Eli told Quiz it was time to go and he promised him he would pass his message on to the crew. Even as Quiz had felt in his heart, there was, indeed, something he yet needed to do for the Doradorans, but that is another story. When Quiz arrived at their island, he was warmly welcomed by all the Doradorans and he found peace and acceptance with his new family.

# Treasure Restored

Forty three years had passed since the town of Harmony was almost entirely destroyed by the visitation of a dragon. The chaos and later dread memory of the event caused a change in the way of life they had lived for generations. Before the attack of the dragon, their role as a center of artwork for gold and silver finery was known throughout the kingdom and the rich came to them with gold and silver they wished to be formed into elaborate works of art.

In one day, however, the terror and destruction wrought by the great Red Dragon caused them all to never again want to keep any gold or silver anywhere near them, fearing that this would only tempt another dragon attack. After so much loss of life and property caused by the rage of the dragon that destroyed their village with fire, the townspeople came to a unanimous decision to switch to farming, even though their customers begged them to work their skills.

The soil was not that productive, but they lived well, even if it was like poverty by comparison. Still, peace with little was better than a prosperity that represented danger from a dragon. Some months later, the one family that defied the will of the town and took in some gold and silver to make jewelry was sadly the victim of another visit from the Red Dragon; their house was burned to the ground when they foolishly tried to resist the attack. The ban on gold and silver and jewelry was never challenged again, and the village had remained at peace for decades.

It was a beautiful morning in the quiet village; there was a soft warmth from the golden sun and the dew was gently suspended over the forests and the fields. All were awake, beginning their chores, and the children were playing and singing in the plaza. As if out of nowhere, a great form swept over the village, temporarily blocking the golden sun and casting an ominous shadow. As they looked up, and saw the dragon, it was the older ones, the ones who remembered, who screamed the loudest. "Run, run for your lives. Abandon the village and do not resist the demon fire beast. Go now, save the children, save yourselves."

The mayor declared: "Elders, we will stay and bring out what little we have as an offering to the dragon and hope for the best. Their fear was multiplied when they saw that it was the same great red dragon from the first attack that was swooping down to land in the plaza. All were prepared for fire and terror and pillaging, but Malpirius just stood there, looking at them.

"Look, they said among themselves, he already has one treasure chest with him, and he comes for more, typical of those evil, greedy worms."

"Normally, I would agree with you about the dragon seeking another chest, but is that not our old community treasure chest he clutches in his wretched claws?" asked the old mayor. "I recognize it and there is our town crest on the side."

"Indeed, it is the same" answered Malpirius. All the treasures that I took from you and your fathers over the years are here; all that and more. They are being restored to you as part of my service to the Old Kingdom, which is to return. The prophecies are true, they are not myth. Prepare the way of the King; seek and restore the old laws of compassion and justice for all. Beware of the greed of treasure. Distribute this with justice, or you will become as the beast I once was. Peace to you, village of Harmon. I leave my mark as a sign that you are now under my protection and my wrath will fall on any who seek to harm you. If you so choose, you may return to your lives as crafters of gold, silver, and jewelry; you will not be attacked.

The great Red Dragon then turned and burned a circle with three lines through it into a solid stone that was alongside the village well. Those who were watching nearby in the forest, not knowing it was a sign of peace, shrieked in terror when they saw the great flames. Then, the great dragon bowed his head, and the villagers stood in amazement.

After distributing the family treasures, the elders noticed there were additional bars of gold and silver in the chest. The extra bars were there, they could only assume, as a gift from the dragon, as he had stated, for dragons were known for their ability to account for every single coin in their troves, and it could not have been an error on his part. The money was used to buy new books for the schools, to create some craftworks to sell, and to rebuild the old bridges.

Once the bridges were restored, some wealthy travelers happened to come through the once impoverished farm village, noticed the elaborate jewelry the villagers wore, and enquired about where they could acquire such fine pieces.

"There are several shops here in town," the travelers were told. "Perak is the silversmith and the Jin Jiang family is known for their works with gold."

The wealthy visitors purchased some of the beautiful artisanship from both shops, and, upon their arrival in the next large town, those townspeople could not help but notice the exquisite jewelry the travelers were wearing, and the question was raised by a noble:

"Excuse me, noble sire, but wherever did you obtain the beautiful silver inlay on your saddle and the harnesses for your horses? They must be heirlooms, for we have not seen this elaborate of craft for decades." Once the word was out, the village of Harmon again became renowned throughout the kingdom for its works with gold and silver. Everything that evil had taken, goodness would restore.

Malpirius continued to restore the treasures to village after village until the villagers throughout the kingdom no longer feared the flight of the dragons but welcomed them and freely offered them gifts when they landed.

"It is strange." thought Malpirius, but I now remember the olden days when we protected the people and it was good. I lament that I was led away by my desire for vengeance. To judge all on the basis of but a few is folly. I attacked the innocent for the sins of others. Now I know that it is far better to be loved than to be feared. I actually find pleasure in these people I used to destroy. What a fool I was. I wonder if I can ever truly be forgiven and restored."

Finally, Malpirius had flown far and wide to find all his treasure troves and had restored all that he could remember, so his vow was fulfilled. Back in his old lair, he stood and pondered what he should do with the rest of the unaccounted for treasures (which were still many).

Suddenly, there was a voice from behind him that said: "the rest of the treasure is yours, my once old enemy. You have done well, and all will be restored."

Malpirius turned to see the great black King of Dragons standing there and he bowed his head low to the ground.

The King of Dragons said:

"Peace to you, Malpirius; all is forgiven, all is restored. Enjoy the service to goodness that was once our place on this earth. There are other dragons that have also been restored to the kingdom;

seek their fellowship and you all will find joy. I must go now, for there is work to be done, but there is something I need to ask of you. There may come a time when I need you to fly by my side again, and I will welcome you in that day. No time for sharing now, I must go." The King of Dragons then bowed his head slightly and flew away.

# Quiz the Protector

On his way to the island of the Dora-dorans, Quiz' flight was interrupted when a little blue bird known as a Pifufu came alongside him. The little bird continually harassed him, chirping and singing, trying to get him to turn aside from his flight. Finally, Quiz relented and followed the Pifufu, who guided him over to a small island where one lone Pifufu was surrounded by five large orange birds that were obviously tormenting him. "Well, this simply will not do," thought Quiz to himself, and he swooped down to get a closer look. He saw one of the large birds jump down and land right on top of the poor little blue bird. The other orange birds were all laughing and taking turns jumping on the bird to get him to sing out a note. When the Pifufu cried out, they all mocked him. "Poor little baby blue, boohoo, and boohoo."

"No this will not do at all," Quiz thought, and he began to prepare his deepest fire breath. He was going to go down there and roast those bullies. Suddenly, the actions of Blue popped into his head; how Blue had frightened him so, without actually hurting him, in order to teach him the lesson that one should not do something just to show that one could.

Quiz dived down and landed right next to the little blue bird and said, "Don't worry, Pifufu, you have a friend in me."

He turned to the orange birds and challenged: "What do you think you are doing to this little guy? You ought to be ashamed of yourselves. Five of you tormenting him (the bird protested, showing her femininity) Oh, excuse me, ma'am, even worse, tormenting her. Not even one of you, being the size you are, should bully something smaller. Shame on you."

One of the orange birds responded: "So what are you going to do about it, oh short, fat miniature winged beach ball type creature?" The other orange birds laughed a raucous laughter at the insult.

The bird continued: "We will have you know that we are the mighty Orange and we rule the skies. Nobody comes into our territory and comes out unpunished. Stand aside, for there are more of us and we can dive bomb you right into oblivion." With that, one of them took off suddenly and flew to a great speed before he came crashing straight into Quiz's chest.

As the Orange bounced off of Quiz and landed upside down some 10 yards away, Quiz asked: "Is that all you got? Now, let me show you what I do to those who commit injustice anywhere, regardless if it is their "territory" or not. All territory belongs to the King, who calls for justice, and you are deserving of wrath."

Quiz looked about and saw a coconut lying on the ground.

"Do you see that coconut there?" He asked.

"Use your imagination and picture that is your pretty little orange fluffy feathered self." Quiz took a deep breath and let loose a terrible blast of fire, instantly roasting the coconut until it exploded in steam. "You, mighty orange birds, are in my territory, and this Pifufu is my friend; shall I let you leave unpunished?" He let them worry for a moment.

"You shall go unpunished, but only if you promise to not bully anymore. I will return and you will be brought to justice for each-and-every wrong you do to any other. Do I make myself clear?" Quiz asked as he snorted more flames from his nostrils.

"Yes, yes, we understand." One of them was gracious enough to thank Quiz for not roasting them for having abused the Pifufu.

# Father and Son

The blacksmith Panday and his son, Sideros, were separated due to the impetuousness that accompanies youth and the lack of bothering to listen to youth that comes with older age. Both father and son were equally at fault, and both knew it.

Good natured, but head strong and impetuous, Sideros had been neglecting his duties at work to spend time on his inventions. Instead of work first and inventions and time away with friends later, Sideros left some customers dissatisfied with the time he took to meet their needs. When his father confronted him, Sideros answered back harshly, stating that his father was just jealous of his inventions and his creativity.

"You judge me wrongly." Panday answered him. "You are very gifted and I am proud of you; you have a marvelous mind and skill with metals, but the reality is you still need to learn about meeting other people's needs more than your own. People count on us to repair their tools so they can work and provide for their families."

Sideros retorted:

"I am tired of all this boring repair stuff." I am going to open my own shop. I don't need you anymore; I have moved on beyond your skills, and I am going off on my own."

"Be careful, my son; you are crossing the line. Selfish pride is the enemy of both truth and love."

Sideros retorted: "That is easy for you to say, blacksmith, you have nothing to be proud of with your little shop here, doing other people's bidding, and not being paid adequately for your services. I will have no more of it."

"Now, you are being prideful. You are not yet knowledgeable enough to run a business on your own. There is still much I need to teach you; you are not as wonderful as you think you are. Don't reason so foolishly, son, you need more discipline."

"So, now I am an undisciplined fool, am I?" Sideros answered. Well, then you are better off without me."

Not meaning it to be an ultimatum, or his last words to his son, Panday retorted, "If you are going to keep that attitude, then yes, I am saying that."

"Fine, then." Sideros responded, and he stormed out of the shop and headed right for the tavern. Once there, he asked around to see if there were a ship leaving port anytime soon. Sideros offered up his skills as a blacksmith and as an apprentice for any trade needed on the ship. As fate would have it, there was a ship leaving the next morning at dawn, and there was a need for his skills, so Sideros signed on. Late that night, he returned to the shop, picked up his tools and the inventions he was working on, and quietly made his way to the docks.

Unfortunately, any adventure that begins with a conflict, becomes a misadventure. Panday awoke, not knowing that his son had taken a spot on a ship that had sailed at dawn. When Sideros did not show up at the shop, Panday felt an empty stillness, and shame at not having been better able to reason with his own son. He went into town to seek him, only to learn the news that he was gone, and his pain multiplied.

When the souls of two people are bonded in love, distance between the two is not a total impediment for communication. Love finds a way. Some many months later, at the very same time his father was painfully and regretfully remembering the argument that separated them, Sideros was far away on the deck of another ship, but under the same star lit sky, experiencing the same remorse. In some sort of synchronicity of their separate thoughts, the two simultaneously recalled their last conversation together.

Both were longing to restore the lost relationship and their souls cried out and touched each other across the sea. Panday ended his thoughts by softly speaking out loud, "I am seeking you, my son, and we shall be restored one to another."

The son, ended his thoughts by softly speaking, "I am coming back home to you, my father, and we shall be together again."

But the path that would bring them back together was not to be an easy one.

# Shipwrecked

That very night the ship Sideros was traveling on met up with a great storm that drove the ship's crew to the point of despair. They feared they would never see their loved ones again. Sadly, for all but three of the entire crew, their premonitions were correct. For three long days and nights they were storm tossed.

Although they had secured the mainsails, the mast was still cracked by the force of the wind and the twisting of the ship's timbers through the waves. It was so dark they could not see that they were being driven onto a rocky shoal, but it would not have mattered anyway; they would not have been able to steer to avoid the catastrophe. Everyone on board could hear the horrible sound of the ship's hull being torn open by the impact. She then ground to a halt and was driven on to her side by the waves.

The storm did not abate, and the waves only grew to crash over the ship as she was held fast against the rocks. The ship was doomed; the only recourse was to seek something that would float and throw oneself into the sea and hope to be pushed by the waves onto a beach landing with a surf. It was dark and terrifying to abandon ship, not knowing if you would survive, or suffer the same fate as thc ship, and die against the rocks. There was no hope in staying aboard, though, the ship was already breaking to pieces under the crashing waves when what was left of the crew threw themselves into the sea.

Sideros had been fortunate to be driven onto the only narrow sandy area on this point of the island. All the other areas where the sea met the land were rocky. He was so exhausted after his ordeal that he fell fast asleep once he had managed to crawl out of the pounding surf and onto higher ground. As he slowly awakened, his mind was foggy. At first, he did not even remember where he was, or that his ship had wrecked. He looked up to see that there were two other crew members higher up on the beach. He slowly crawled up to them to see if they, too, had survived. Both were saved, but like him, were not in good shape. Their first need was fresh water, or they would not live long. All the salt water they had swallowed had drained them, and the temperature on the shore in the sun was over 100 degrees. Together they got up to assess the situation.

Before they moved inland, though, they thought it would be best to check to see if any supplies from the ship had washed ashore. As they looked out at the broken ship on the rocks, and the surrounding reef, they noticed that there was only one small opening through the rocks to pass through safely, and they had mercifully been washed through there.

They knew that it was unlikely that there were any other survivors. The three agreed to split up, but to only travel some 400-500 yards distance before coming back together. The helmsman, Kormilar, looked to the right of the little cove they were in, Sideros looked to the left and Yunqi, the youngest, climbed to the top of the rocks to see what he could see.

Amazingly, Sideros found his wooden toolbox had washed ashore. He had just cleaned it out, so all his heavier tools and larger bars of iron were not in it, making the box more buoyant. Inside the box were some of his inventions, a small pulley, some small bars of metal, and a small bellows he could use to create a small kiln. Kormilar returned, having found nothing of use in his search.

When Yunqi came down from the cliff, he said he thought he had seen smoke coming from an area not too far away, and they all agreed that they should cautiously head in that direction. They also agreed they would remain hidden just in case the natives of this island had a habit of consuming the Lusan flesh of those they met. However, if they could not find a source of water, they would be forced to go into the village or to face death by dehydration.

On the way towards the village, the three had found no water, and were now beyond desperate. Their tongues were swollen, and it was even getting more difficult for them to breathe. They knew they would die of thirst if they did not get water; all they could do was hope the villagers were not cannibals. Yunqi joked that maybe they would even feed them and fatten them up before they ate them.

The same storm that had driven their ship onto the rocks had also torn into the village, bringing tragedy. The hut in which the witch doctor lived was near an old palm tree; a tree that was felled on to his hut that night by the winds.

By all appearances, the witch doctor had been killed. However, the head wound he sustained, though serious, only knocked him out, causing him to suffer complete amnesia. When he was set out for burial the next day, while the villagers were preparing the ceremonies, he had awakened, and wandered off into the jungle alone. When the villagers turned around and the "dead" doctor was gone, they considered it a fearsome omen. Only some dread judgment or a more powerful witch doctor could have caused his death and disappearance.

The villagers were petrified, and so distracted that they did not notice the approach of the three shipwrecked foreigners approaching their village. The villagers were on their knees before their idol, seeking what they must do to appease the gods and keep them from delivering more wrath upon them.

The appearance of the three aliens could only mean one thing to the villager's primitively religious minds – everything was fine until these people showed up, therefore they had evidently brought the tragedy with them. They would have to be sacrificed for the good of the village. Sideros and his friends soon found themselves on the wrong end of the spears and arrows pointed at them. The islanders appeared to be fierce warriors, but simultaneously they appeared frightened.

"One thing is for sure, said Sideros. Betchya they have never seen a black Lusan. They seem kinda nervous."

"Black, Brown or White, we are gonna die," joked Yunqi through parched lips.

Noticing that none of their weapons were of metal, Sideros hoped to capitalize on their lack of technical knowledge. All Sideros could think of, although it was not much to go on, was to try and 'wow' the islanders with a "Jack in the Box" device he had made. It was in his box of tools that he had not wanted to abandon because he knew they could come in handy if they survived. Sideros set the box down, knelt in the sand, and motioned the warriors toward him.

The warriors were apprehensive and suspected some danger, but Sideros opened his toolbox so that they could see the contents. There were obviously no weapons there, and the islanders were curious. Sideros hoped that the small amount of salt water that had entered the box did not ruin anything- it had not. Still, what he did not know was that the salt and the humidity and the heat had melted the soft red paint on the face of the "Jack" in his Jack- in- the- box.

Sideros slowly withdrew the box with one hand while he kept his other hand in the air in surrender, and then motioned for them all to sit down in the sand. He placed the Jack-in-the-box on his lap and slowly cranked the handle.

At the sound of the first musical notes, the islanders jumped back in awe, but as he continued, they were fascinated and drew closer to see the little music box. Unfortunately, the face on the little figure that popped out, because of the melted red paint, looked quite macabre and the villagers could only interpret the little puppet in the box to be the captured soul of their witch doctor, an action that this person of evidently greater power had accomplished. They treated the new arrivals with fear and reverence and brought the three into the village. The mysterious visitors were provided with all manner of food and gifts; the most welcome items were the beverages they were served to slake their thirst.

The village chief ordered that the witch doctor's goods should be given to Sideros, who knew that he must accept the gifts. Kormilar and Yunqi stuck close to him and he asked them if they had any special skills that would impress their hosts, so they could be ensured an honored status in the village.

Kormilar, the navigator, could, of course, speak of the stars and celestial movements even without language, and Yunqi had learned some simple sleight of hand magic tricks in order to win free drinks; he also knew the formula for gunpowder, if the raw elements were available. In fact, he had been working on a waterproof container for extra powder, and just happened to have a small container of it on his person, sealed with wax as waterproofing.

That evening, as they were gathered around the village fire, Yunqui stood up, made an elaborate show of making a medallion he wore "disappear" and "reappear" magically. Then, once he had their attention, he mumbled some words and threw a small amount of powder into the fire with a shout. The effect on the villagers was utter astonishment and instant status was granted to him.

Although Kormilar was not aware of it, the movement of some asteroids was perfect for this night, and as he stood and began gesturing towards the stars, a meteoroid shower shot across the horizon. Truly, the islanders assumed, the gods had come to visit their village.

Kormilar was amused by the coincidence and did not have to tell his companions that the appearance was totally serendipitous. Yunqi quipped with a smile, "You just had to outshine my trick with the gunpowder, didn't you?"

Sideros turned to his companions and stated,

"Now we are responsible to use their over estimation of who we are for good; we have a great responsibility here and we must never abuse this power. We must teach them that we come to represent mercy and justice for all people." But how to accomplish this with the language barrier was difficult.

The following day, Sideros decided that they should swim out to the remains of their ship to see if there was anything useful they could float back to the island. The seas were calm that morning as they swam out to see what tools or supplies they could find that would help them build a small boat and escape from the island to get back home. Some of the islanders, who were expert swimmers, followed along out of curiosity. With some degree of luck, the small cargo crane with pulleys was still there, and with the aid of a small hand ax they found, they chopped out several sections of deck planking to make a raft, and floated it back to the village. They swam back to the ship where they found some line, tied it around a cargo net and swam just the line back to shore. Then they used the line to haul several nets back to shore; these nets would come in handy later.

Over the following weeks, Sideros showed the islanders how the pulley could be used to lift heavy objects; it was used to repair many damaged huts and to create new ones with less struggle on the part of all. Sideros also showed them how to build a kiln that they could use to fire bricks. Although he only had a little bit of iron, he showed them his skills with metals, and even created a large, lethal spear tip for the chief. They had never seen iron before and they were amazed at the size, weight and sharpness of the spear point. The gift was well received - it was important to keep on the good side of the village chief.

As they interacted with the people, the three recorded the words they needed to learn. By creating a dictionary, they picked up the language fairly easily and began to get to know them. The phonetic dictionary was used to help the people develop a written language. After some six months living there, Sideros and Kormilar had decided that, as nice as it was to be treated like gods, they would prefer to get back to their lives as normal people. They missed home and family. Yunqi, though, did not share their dreams of escape. He had fallen in love with a beautiful young maiden who was also in love with him.

As the weeks rolled on, the three were communicating better with the islanders. Sideros noted that the poles that held the huts up, especially the large community hut, were made of a strong, dense wood that could be used to construct a small craft for their escape; he made it understood they wanted to know where on the island these trees grew. The natives agreed to show them the trees, and the next day they started back into the interior of the island.

Although they only had the hand ax, they were able to, with difficulty, fell some good trees. With help from the strong natives, some good sections were ready to be hauled back. Sideros had gone ahead a way into the interior and sought to have some natives follow him to another grove of trees by a river. They, however, steadfastly refused.

One of the natives stopped him and forbade him to go farther. "Kotu Yilan, Kotu Yilan," he said.

Sideros knew the word Kotu meant evil, but he did not know the meaning of the word Yilan.

The islander drew what could only be described as a giant serpent in the dirt and made signs that it was at least forty feet long and would attack them if they approached the river. Pointing to the opening of a cave some 15 feet above the river, he indicated the monster lived in there.

Sideros was intrigued. How could such a beast live? What did it eat? The islander indicated it ate the wild goats on the island, and if provoked in any way or became hungry, it would attack the villagers.

In their foolish fear, the villagers would even take a young Lusan to the edge of the river to sacrifice to the serpent god to (they thought) appease it. A native showed them an altar on which they would lay their heavily sedated sacrificial victim. It was surrounded by religious symbols and a shrine. Sideros could not even conceive of such an act, although he did know of idolatry in the ancient times. One thing, he knew, he could not allow such a thing to occur while he had any say whatsoever.

By some horrible coincidence, although the great serpent had not been disturbed by the harvesting of trees, that night it came slithering into the village, destroying many homes and eating several of the unfortunate goats that were tied up.

The people themselves had been able to flee, but the chief ordered that a young maiden would have to be sacrificed in order to appease the evil serpent.

At first, Yunqui was unwilling to interfere with the decision for a sacrifice. Even though he was morally opposed, he did not want to jeopardize his status in the community so that he could stay on the island and live with his new-found love, Sulana.

Sideros was most adamant that Yunqui join him and Kormilar in standing up against any Lusan sacrifice as long as they had any say. In fact, they were willing to stand up in battle, risking their lives to defend the next innocent victim.

Yunqui argued, "Should we really be interfering in the culture of these people? This is their religion and they have followed it for generations. Who are we to come along and tell them they should change?"

Sideros answered Yunqui: "Can you not hear what you are saying? By your words, you are justifying the killing of the innocent. Just because it is a religion, it does not make it right. Even if it is their religion, it is wrong and it is a great sin against the Source that guides us all to know that life is sacred, and especially the life of the innocent. Please think long and hard about what you are saying and the great wrong you will be allowing to happen, and the sad fact that you are doing this so you can protect your standing in the community."

As fate would have it, the chief cast lots to see who should be sacrificed and the lot fell upon Sulana, Yunqi's beloved, to be sacrificed the next full moon, which was a fortnight away. Yunqi, of course, had a precipitous change in philosophy and was now ready to stand in battle and be killed rather than see his love be killed in a useless sacrifice.

Sideros and Kormilar calmed him down and proposed an alternative plan.

"So, now you are ready to fight, are you? There is another way to solve this. Rather than battle with the natives, why don't we battle with the Kotu Yilan and kill it? That way, we could show the tragedy of human sacrifice to something that was not a god at all, and we can further point them to the true Source of life."

Knowing well that the serpent would be bloated and in need of rest in order to digest the village goats it had just eaten, they knew where to find the beast; in its cave. Sideros asked Yunqi if he thought there was another cargo net they could retrieve, and maybe even locate the ship's swivel gun, (small cannon). If they were going to go on a giant snake hunt, they would need that thing. They all headed back to the remains of ship, this time to conduct their most important search.

As Yunqi swam under the planks of the ship, he noticed that a small powder keg was still intact; it was floating, but it had been trapped underneath some planks that would have to be removed in order to free it. Now, all they needed was to locate the swivel gun. After several dives, Yunqi could see it, but it was too deep for him to hold his breath long enough to free it. He came back to the surface and noticed that there were some islanders in the water that were watching him. They all got back on the wreck and Yunqui asked them to take a line down to the broken section that held the gun and tie it up so they could haul it aboard. The natives did not know what they were retrieving, but their skills as free divers were more than up to the task. They easily overcame the depths and secured a line.

Sideros and Kormilar braced a broken section of a yardarm under a section of the rail and used one of the sail hoisting pulleys to bring the plank and small cannon to the surface. It took them all day, but they were able to get it back to the island where they could have more time and better tools to cut it free from the broken plank.

The islanders, of course, had no idea what all the fuss was about. "What was the value of this strange shaped tube that they had retrieved from the wreck?" they asked themselves.

Once it was free, Sideros, who was big and heavy enough (just barely) to handle the recoil of the gun, was ready to give it a go, and he knew what target he was going to use to demonstrate the power of the cannon. There was a shrine in the village with an idol dedicated to the great serpent. They were cautious to not give the weapon too heavy of a load of powder, and they used smooth, heavy river stones as projectiles.

Sideros called the chief up near the gun and explained in their language with simple terms:

"Up to now, we have not interfered with your religion. All people are free to worship as best they understand, insomuch as it does not involve injustice to others. Justice must be equal for all. Our conscience dictates that we must now interfere to protect the innocent. Sacrificing a life to a giant serpent that is no god is not justice. We will not allow Sulana to die." Sideros continued:

"The Kotu Yilan will be killed because it has killed others and you have made it a sacrificial god. A sound like great thunder will come from this gun. You are chief, you may touch this fire to this part of the gun and it will destroy whatever it is pointed at." Yunqi put his fingers in his ears to demonstrate to all the islanders what to do.

The chief casually touched the fuse off. He, nor any other islander was at all prepared for the noise, nor for the destruction. When the smoke cleared there was pandemonium; even the bravest warriors ran or anxiously looked about, but Sideros called them back to show that the idol and all the shrine was blasted away. "There will be no more sacrifices. Tomorrow, send only your bravest warriors to help us kill the serpent." Sideros told the chief.

That night, the chief wrestled with his belief systems. Had he been wrong to order those sacrifices? Why was his village chosen to be the center of the war of some gods? What if their Kotu Yilan god were more powerful? Would his village, his people, be destroyed by its vengeance? He worried all night long, even contemplating the capture of the three new powerful visitors, but in the end, he surrendered to fate to decide who would win the battle. If the snake god won, then he could always sacrifice Sulana, and one of the visitors to appease its wrath.

Because the snake's river ran through a ravine with sheer cliffs on both sides. Their first plan was to lower Sideros, who would be holding the loaded ship's gun, over the side of the cliff above the serpent's cave so he could blast it in the head while it was sleeping. If the snake were awakened, Sideros could call out to be immediately raised out of danger.

As a back-up plan, Sideros had noticed that across from the cave, there was a tall tree on the opposite cliff. By felling that tree, it would create a bridge between the two sides; a bridge from which some of the ship's pulleys could be secured. Sideros planned to quietly drop some lines through some pulleys, secure them to three cargo nets tied together that would be weighted down to the bottom of the river where they would be hidden. If the serpent dropped from the cave into the river, they would raise the nets and trap him.

Once all the preparations were made by the three visitors, the time had come and Sideros was silently lowered down to the entrance of the cave. As he moved his torch to see in the darkness, he saw two giant, cold steely eyes glaring out at him. "Pull me up, pull me up, pull me up!" He screamed in terror. His legs had just cleared the entrance when the giant head of the monster shot forth, mouth open, showing horrendous, jagged fangs and backwards slanting teeth.

The beast slithered out into the river, and Sideros called for the nets to be raised. There was just enough room in the nets to hold the length of the monster. Sideros had run across the tree bridge and aimed the gun down towards the serpent. He needed some support from behind so he would not be blown off the tree by the recoil of the swivel gun. The serpent thrashed around inside the net, but the pulleys held firm. Sideros let loose a blast from the gun which caught the serpent with a load of projectiles. Unfortunately, they did not hit their mark behind the head, nor did they hit any vital organs. The serpent was enraged, and although it was trapped in the nets, it managed to push its head out through a small opening at the top and strike out at those on the log. Some of them, to include Sideros with the cannon, fell into the river below. One of the pulley ropes had fallen free of the net, but it was still secured to the tree above.

Yunqi was not going to allow the serpent to live, for he knew it would result in the death of his beloved Sulana. As the serpent struggled to crawl out of the top opening, Yunqi pulled in the rope, and calculated the distance of the arc that his next move would require. As the monster turned its head away to look for another opening, Yunqi reached out for a spear and was ready to swing forward on a trajectory that he hoped would provide the right distance and the requisite force to drive the spear into the base of the monster's skull. Those who were watching could not believe their eyes. Yunqi, they thought, had no chance against the beast with that spear.

From behind him, Yunqi heard the voice of the chief, who had suddenly run across the log while raising the iron headed spear that Sideros had made for him as a gift. He pushed Yunqi aside, smiled and swung out to meet his destiny. As fate would have it, the trajectory and momentum were perfect and the chief drove the spear home, deep into the soft part behind the serpent's skull. The great beast jerked its head twice, with the chief still holding onto the spear, then quivered and fell still.

A great cheer rose from the crowd that had gathered to watch the great contest, as the brave warriors, led by their chief, stood by the body of the serpent that had once ruled over them. After the beast was staked down to keep it from moving, even while dead (which snakes will do), it was skinned, although with great difficulty. Everyone was allowed to cut off sections of meat to roast over the village fire that evening in a huge celebration which became an annual festival. The skin was so long and broad that it was even used to make light and swift canoes to travel the river, which was now free of the monster. The skull was preserved and set atop the hut of the chief.

Months had passed and Kormilar and Sideros had finished constructing their vessel; it was time to leave. Sideros was making one last search of the island for fresh food that they could take with them when they sailed upon the next day. As he was walking along the river, he chanced upon someone getting a drink down by the river's edge. As Sideros approached him, he seemed frightened, but Sideros spoke in his language, (as best he could) and called him friend. Sideros offered him some of the smoked meat he had prepared, and he smiled as he tasted it. At the same time the stranger noticed the amulet that was the symbol for the village medicine man hanging from Sideros' neck, Sideros noticed that under the his hair line there was a great scar.

Sideros deduced this was the doctor that had "disappeared". Sideros took the amulet and placed it around his neck. In broken language, Sideros said:

"You are the doctor; your village needs you. You were injured, but you are now healed. Remember". Sideros placed his hands on his head and said again, "Remember."

The doctor looked down at the amulet just as the sun caught it perfectly – causing it to glow magically with a beautiful light and dropped to his knees as everything came flooding back to him. "I remember" he said. "It is time to take my place again."

"Not quite yet." Sideros cautioned. "Sit down, my friend. Your heart is good and pure, but your mind has been in error. You have done your best, but you have believed in many things that are not true and good. There is only one Source of life to be worshipped. I was sent to this island to teach this. We have killed the Kotu Yilan that you made sacrifices to. This should not have been, for it was not just and good to sacrifice an innocent young Lusan to a beast because you feared its power. The old ways must be changed, there will be no more idols."

Do you see, this hat; this is part of the skin from the Kotu Yilan that you once sacrificed to. We, along with your chief, killed it and ate it. Even the meat you just ate is its flesh. It was no god and your beliefs caused injustice. When you go back to the village, you must weigh all decisions by the rule of love and justice, for so it must be. Your people need you and your wisdom for life, but follow no god or rule that does not call for justice for all. I have been here almost a year and you were kept away for this season for a greater purpose. I am leaving tomorrow. Today, I will take you back to your village and I will surrender my position back over to you. Do you agree to live and teach as I have said?"

"Yes, yes, I do." replied the doctor.

"Good; you will find that your people have changed also."

As the two approached the village, one of the warriors saw the two of them together and began to signal with the drums:

*One was taken when the other came near, He came to teach us not to fear,*
*Now he leaves and the first returns and we all shall live by the lessons learned.*
*Justice for all, for all are brothers.*
*There is only one Source and we follow no others.*

The villagers wondered about the meaning of the drums' message until they saw the two medicine sages together and all were amazed. As promised, Sideros relinquished his post and all were glad to see the restoration. If all the other things he did were not enough, in surrendering to, and not killing the one who was weaker and vulnerable, Sideros confirmed the message he had been teaching. The greater power that loves is greater than any that seeks to rule by fear. The chief finally surrendered his heart to change his ways. There would be no more sacrifice and no idol worship.

The next morning the entire village, to include Yunqi and his newly pregnant wife Sulana, saw the two visitors off with prayers and the best of wishes for a safe journey.

# Blue to the Rescue

After leaving their friend Yunqui on the is-land and sailing out to sea to seek a way home, Sideros and Kormilar were still of good cheer. They had been at sea for just over a week, guided by Kormilar's excellent navigational skills, when their vessel was hit by some unidentified large sea creature that apparently thought it needed to protect its territory. As it turns out, the wooden vessel was a tougher surface than the creature thought, for it delivered only one attack and then left them alone. Still, the impact was enough to cause a break in the seal between two planks. At first, the leak was rather small, but it continued to widen.

"Did we bring anything like a bucket for bailing water?" Kormilar asked.

"Just my fancy hat I made from the serpent" Sideros responded. "It is not much, but it will have to do. You are the navigator; how long would we have to keep swimming if our little vessel here were to break apart?"

"Oh, I'd say about three weeks in any given direction. Not that that would matter, the heat and dehydration would take us long before then, or maybe the sharks."

Sideros looked off to the port side of their little vessel and noticed one rather large triangular fin slicing through the water near them. "I do wish you had not said the 'S' word." joked Sideros. Their 'friend' had been with them now for three days. "Bailing it is, then, for as long as possible."

That night, while they were fast asleep, both were awakened by the shifting movement of the planks, and water came gushing through where one plank had broken loose and was missing entirely. The situation was bleak. But then, of all the strange things, they heard what sounded like music. Some distance away, they saw the lights of the Karu Mar on the water. The crew was up late, celebrating their return to homeport. There was dancing and storytelling and some degree of consumption of the ship's store of beverages.

Kormilar studied the tack and speed of the Karu Mar and calculated a trajectory that could bring their vessel within hailing distance. Their boat was no match for the speed of the Karu Mar, and it was hampered by the missing plank. It was going to be a close call if they made it at all.

Both knew to save their voices and not begin yelling too soon. There was no way they could be heard over the sound of the celebrations. There was no use trying to light a fire. The box that contained the materials was turned upside down when the plank cut loose; they would have to hope for the best.

Twenty minutes on a perfect line of intercept later, Sideros and Kormilar were close enough to begin yelling and making noise with the hope of being heard. Being seen was not likely; they were facing the moon, so their vessel would not be silhouetted and easily spotted. Besides, who would be looking out to the side of the ship with all the excitement going on?"

Sideros and Kormilar were now as close as they were going to get in order to be rescued. They both yelled at the top of their lungs, but they were not heard, and the Karu Mar was slipping away. As it turned out, Rohani was down in the hold talking with Fred about other adventures when her big ears picked up the last frustrated sounds of Sideros banging a board against the raft and screaming, "Why don't you hear us?" She looked out a port hole and saw the small vessel drifting away behind them.

"Fred," she asked, "did you not hear them calling for help? Why are you not doing something?"

"Oh, I am doing something, but this one is not my assignment" he responded.

Rohani asked in wonder, "Not your assignment? So, you are going to just sit here and let them suffer and probably die? What kind of Angel are you?"

"Sit here is exactly what I am going to do, Rohani. Just because you can do something does not mean that you should do it or that you have to do it. They are not going to suffer, and they are not going to die. Someone else is supposed to pick this one up."

"Just any someone? Well, I am not going to do nothing, I am going topside to sound the alarm."

"More power to you, Rohani," he said. "You go, girl."

Before Rohani could get to the main deck to sound the alarm, Blue, who was in the water under the ship had already heard the sound of the boards thumping nearby. He swam over in the direction of the source of the sound and surfaced to investigate just in time to see the raft breaking apart, and he saw them going into the water some 80 yards astern. Sideros and Kormilar were convinced they would be eaten by the sharks and were terrified as they continued to scream for help, but the Karu Mar kept sailing away.

Rohani started sounding the alarm, which caused the lookout to focus on the water rather than on the party on board.

Just before Blue could get to the helpless sailors, one of his arms was grabbed by the sharp teeth of a giant shark. Blue rolled up the shark in one of his arms and continued to reach out to grab hold of Sideros and Kormilar and lift them out of the water, in case there were other sharks, and more sharks there were. Another of Blue's arms was bitten, but it did not deter him from his mission. By this time, the ship had located the survivors by the light of the moon, but none knew that Blue was already involved and was in danger himself while rescuing them.

As the ship approached, the lookout noticed that the people he had seen were seemingly floating eleven feet above the water. As they neared, the crew could see that Blue's long arms were holding them aloft, and they also noticed that Blue was thrashing about on the surface of the water.

"Prepare the swivel gun," the lookout cried. "Blue is in trouble."

Blue's first priority was to affect a rescue, so he kept them in the air while he picked up another shark and sent it flying. When the Karu Mar came alongside them, Blue reached up and placed the two sailors onto the deck of the ship. The gunner was able to get one well-placed shot on one of the sharks, and blood filled the water. Predictably, some of the sharks turned on their wounded comrade and began to tear him apart.

Sadly, Blue was pulled under the water in his battle with the sharks. Minutes passed, and then a half hour, and then several hours, but there was no sign of Blue and no sign of the sharks. Eli ordered that they were to hold their position and to circle the area as needed because the ocean there was entirely too deep for an anchor. Sunrise came and the Chief asked how much longer Eli wanted to remain.

"Until we see the end of this, one way or another," Eli responded.

It was only natural that stories about Blue were being told among the crew as they passed the time awaiting to learn of his fate. No one yet had sought the identities of the rescued. It was dark when Blue set them on board and everyone was too busy with the affairs at hand. Furthermore, the two did not want to interfere, so they just stood at the rail with the others to wait to learn the fate of their rescuer – and of course, they had no idea why a giant octopus named Blue would be a part of this ship's crew and be so beloved.

Finally, there was enough light for the faces of those rescued to be clearly seen, but Panday had gone below to work on sharpening another harpoon to help Blue if more sharks came, so he did not realize that his son had been rescued and the son did not know his father was on board.

There was some small talk and introductions among the rescued and the crew when Sideros mentioned his story. Eli pulled him aside and asked him if he would go below and ask to see if he could help the ship's blacksmith with some repairs.

"It's the least I could do for the rescue" Sideros said. As he came down the ladder, he asked aloud "Is the blacksmith here?"

"Come forward and to starboard and you will find him." Panday looked up just in time to see his son approaching. Sideros recognized his father and the two ran to embrace. No words of apology were exchanged, just tears and a shared expression of joy at seeing each other again.

"My quest is ended" they simultaneously said , and they hugged again. As they both headed topside, and before they had even come on deck, Eli stated, "Behold, father and son are reunited, even as it was promised."

From below deck, Fred said, "Another prophecy fulfilled; the clock is winding down."

"Do you mean to say that Blue just rescued Panday's son, the one he has been looking for this entire voyage?" asked Old Bill. A warm smile crossed his face. "Well, that is amazing, even if I do say so myself."

"Yes, you did just say so yourself," Sadik quipped. "And, I caught you smiling."

"Don't get used to it." Bill said with a smile.

This was no sooner said than Blue finally came back to the surface. The Chief shouted out, "Three cheers for Blue, shark killer and hero," and the whole crew shouted it out. It was only then that they noticed that Blue was severely wounded. Blue reached up and pulled himself onto the deck, careful to not swamp the vessel. "Permission to come aboard, Captain," he said. "I think I need to rest up here for a while, if I could."

Because he was so huge, Blue did not normally put his weight and bulk on the ship, but this was needful. Blue had two arms severed about half-way up, and two others were severely wounded. Rohani cried out with compassion,

"Oh, Blue, you poor dear; just lie down here and we will take care of you."

"Don't worry about it too much." Blue said; "my arms will grow back, which is better than I can say than for the dead sharks they are still wrapped around."

"You see, even if some of my arms get severed from my body, they still kinda have a mind of their own and they will just keep holding on to those killers. Still, there were two other huge killers and it took me a while to win, but there were more arms on me than there were sharks, and I had time on my hands, err arms. Anyway, time was on my side. You see, I just grabbed them and held them and then I sank to the deep cold bottom and held them all tied up. Without being able to move, they could breathe, but not breathe very well at all, and I knew the cold and their slowed breathing would sap them of energy. I could breathe more efficiently and thermoregulate better. Once they were all played out, I came back up – sorry for the delay. For now, could you guys just patch me up and let me warm up in the sun for a while?" And with that, Blue fell fast asleep on deck while everyone tended to his wounds.

On the way back to their respective home islands, the crew plied Sideros and Kormilar with many questions about their voyage and adventures, and the two of them marveled at the adventures the others had experienced on the Karu Mar.

# Homeward Bound

T he return trip on the Karu Mar went more quickly than all had imagined. As promised, the soldiers from the Isle of Corbatanos were given the opportunity to get off on the first habitable island to start a new life, most all did, but a few chose to stay on the Karu Mar to go back to Mekaikki, the home of the original crew.

The days and nights were spent laughing and reliving their old adventures together. Sometimes a story grows fonder when retold from another's perspective. When each shared his take on a given adventure and what he had learned, it added new depth and meaning to the events. It was always funny to hear someone say, "Well that is not how I remember it" or "That is not the way you told the story last time." (all in jest, of course).

One night, Eli announced that their adventures together were coming to an end. On the next day, Kormilar would be returned to his island, and within seven more nights, the original crew would be back home. Rohani and Sadik had made the decision to stay with Barnabas, Bartholomew, Bill and Jeffery, the Sheriff, and Panday and Sideros on Mekaikki. Rohani said she was ready for some fresh grass and maybe some nice cool mud to roll in.

Sadik agreed to work with Sideros and Panday at their re-opened blacksmith shop to earn some money to buy a place of his own. After all, if he were to meet a lady Chimono, he would need a place for her to stay when they were married. Still, all agreed that they would answer Eli's call if he needed them.

Blue decided to stay with the Karu Mar and sail along for more adventures.

"Really," he stated, I live in the water anyway, so why not have a traveling companion that could provide pickled fish?" The arms the sharks had torn off were growing back and he was feeling stronger.

Adalet and Kagayaku were excited to travel with Captain Eli back to the island of Hang-gu. Eli was curious to hear the full story of the encounter between Malpirius and Horace, and he wanted to see Melissa fully restored to health. Eli also knew that there was a destiny for Melissa and Adalet. He knew they would play a role in the final battle and the restoration of the kingdom.

Their friendship was a perfect match: Melissa had always wanted a sister, and Adalet needed a family. She could not return to her kingdom because to do so would only endanger all of her people. She did, however, dispatch a secret message to the King's council, informing them that she was well, but must remain hidden. The King and Queen, she informed them ,were being held captive by Prince Toh-Kali, who had sunk their ship and kidnapped them.

One night, Barnabas was up late, pacing the deck as he thought about why he was given the sword of power and wondered about when he would be called upon to use it. Furthermore, he wondered if he ever did need to use it, would he find the courage to do so?

Sadik noticed he was concerned about something and asked; "Hey, why the worried look on your face?"

Barnabas replied. "All my life I have wanted to be a peacemaker; I am not a warrior. Why did this sword come to me?"

Sadik responded: "Did you ever consider that someone who had a warrior's heart might very well abuse the power of the sword, maybe use it too hastily, and that this is why it came to an encourager like you? There is a reason you were chosen. I have thought about this myself. It is good that you have not had to use that sword; peace is better than war. When the time comes you will know."

"Well, I am in no hurry to use it, I just do not want to be unworthy of the trust." answered Barnabas.

# An Unwelcome Return

The next morning, the Karu Mar was sailing into the harbor at Mekaikki. They all noticed that few people were out in the town square and there were few windows open to the street and to the sea.

*"Something does not feel right here, there is something wrong, I fear."* stated the sheriff.

It was then they noticed the black flags of Prince Toh-Kali flying from the top of the Mayor's home.

"This cannot be," said Barnabas.

"Have we sailed so long and had so many adventures that we come home to find more trouble instead of a place to rest?"

"We will not stand for this, not at our home." shouted the others. "Prepare the cannons, prepare for battle. Those servants of Toh-Kali have gone too far this time."

"If one of our loved ones has been harmed, there will be blood in the streets." shouted old Bill. "Sheriff, call the ship to arms, and let us answer this indignity."

Captain Eli told Bill to stand down and gathered the crew together as they entered the harbor.

"Fighting evil on another's land is one thing. You have all proven yourselves strong in the defense of the homeland of others. It may be that you will now have to defend your own. Evil, I must sadly say, pushes its ugly presence everywhere people are too weak to withstand it. But, be careful; up to now you have acted bravely and with honor, so do not let your love for your homeland cause you to take vengeance instead of delivering justice. To spill innocent blood, or to spill blood in cold vengeance will erase every authority to act in the right. Do not act until we have fully assessed the situation."

As the ship was being tied to the pier, an awesome group of soldiers clad in black approached them with their weapons at the ready. They were all between six and seven feet tall. Their captain stepped onto the ship without requesting permission and defiantly stated:

"So, here comes the great Captain Eli and his misfit crew. We have been warned that you have special powers and have defeated powerful adversaries. Therefore, we have prepared ourselves to deal with you. We have you at a distinct disadvantage; that is, we also understand that you have a weakness that we are prepared to exploit. For some pitiful reason or another, you actually care about what happens to other people. We do not suffer from such a weakness and consider them to simply be collateral damage in any and all of our conflicts. So, here are my demands; either you and your goodie- goodie crew turn this ship around and leave this place, or there will be more collateral damage than you can ever imagine."

"We are the Herzlos, Prince Toh-Kali's special warriors who obey with no questions and care not for any of the consequences resulting from his right to rule over all. You have but one minute to comply, or we will begin the slaughter of these townspeople. Your rescue mission will become a failed mission of death. To let you know how serious we are, we will start with this pretty little girl right here in front of you, as an example."

Up at the end of the pier towards the town, two soldiers stepped forward, holding a beautiful young girl and another drew his sword to strike.

"You have sixty seconds from now to start fitting your ship for immediate departure or the little girl loses her head."

Suddenly, a young Lusan leapt forward from the Karu Mar and onto the pier in front of the warriors. He was dwarfed by their enormous size and was armed only with a sword, which was not even drawn from it's scabbard.

"What a bunch of low-life stinking cowards you are. Look at you, hiding behind a little girl. Are you not brave enough to face a challenger? Are you so weak that the only one you can kill is an unarmed little girl? What is more, I think you are, every mother's son of you, as ugly as you are cowardly."

The warriors were shocked that such a small challenger, with no armor, would dare to insult them, and they were momentarily stopped. Barnabas continued:

"And you, o pusillanimous Herzlos captain, you do not scare me one bit. I challenge you to a duel to the death. If you are not too frightened, that is, you despicable worm."

Barnabas' challenge was met only with the sounds of laughter: the laughter of derision from the Herzlos and the laughter of amazement from the crew of the Karu Mar because they had never seen him insult anyone. Then there was the joyful laughter of Captain Eli, who loved to see destiny unfolding.

"Young fool, I could have overlooked your challenge as inconsequential, but your insults have sealed your fate. I have half a mind to have my archers kill you where you stand, but you have made this personal, so mortal combat it will be, and I will not make your death quick nor easy on you."

Barnabas replied: "You have spoken truly. You do, indeed, have only half a mind, and that is on your best day, I do not doubt. Bring your worst. I also will not make your death quick, but this is because I will give you a chance to accept mercy at my hand."

The evil captain drew his sword and swung low to injure Barnabas, but the younger one was too quick, and when he drew his sword, it shone a radiant blue light. The next blow from the Herzlos captain was swift, but it was blocked, and the Herzlos' blade was shattered to pieces when it struck the sword of power. In an instant, his foe drew a shorter sword and lunged again, but this attack was also futile. Barnabas dodged to the side and used the flat of his sword to strike the Herzlos square on the buttocks, lifting him off his feet and

275

propelling him in the air. He was sent flying right into the cold water of the harbor.

The celebration from the Karu Mar was short lived. A shout from one of the soldiers screamed "Archers, release." Seven deadly arrows were sent in flight towards Barnabas, but he raised his sword and all disintegrated when they ran into a glowing blue force field surrounding him. This did not deter the soldiers from their treachery, however. While two soldiers charged him, the two holding the little girl captive announced:

"We warned you of the consequences, this girl's life is now forfeit." The soldier holding the knife against her raised the weapon to plunge it into her heart. Barnabas' heart fell sick as he recognized the situation was hopeless; there was no way he could intervene in time. All he could do was scream "Nooo" in despair, trying his best to fight his way through the wall of soldiers between him and the girl.

Unbeknownst to all, however, a rescue had already been secured. As soon as Blue had seen that the little girl's life was in jeopardy, he began his plan to save her. Over and over Blue played a scenario in his mind; the only problem was that it necessitated perfect camouflage. Though he did not know it, Blue's inability to camouflage had resulted from his fear of failure; he had failed to believe in himself and his ability to perfect a camouflage.

"OK, I admit I cannot do this for myself, but I know I can do this for that innocent little girl," Blue said to himself, and that was the key to ensuring the success of his mission.

From the bottom of the harbor, Blue slowly reached forth his arms and willed them to blend perfectly in with the color and even the texture of the ground leading out of the water, up to the pier, and even of the pier itself.

"For you, little girl, I am the ground, I am the pier, I am the ground, I am the pier."

Nobody, unless he was intently watching and anticipating the movement along the ground would have been able to detect Blue's efforts. Before the action with Barnabas had begun, Blue's perfectly camouflaged arms had crawled up behind the two soldiers that were holding the girl, and another arm was waiting to grab the girl.

When Blue saw Barnabas would be unable to rescue her, he swiftly and simultaneously yanked the two soldiers up by their ankles and abruptly flung them into the air. They fell and crashed through the roof of the tavern. With another arm,

Blue swiftly wrapped up the girl and pulled her up over his head and onto the safety of the deck of the Karu Mar where she was welcomed with hugs and cheers and laughter.

When Barnabas had seen the rescue completed, he turned his focus back to the fray. What happened next froze them all with fear. The evil group had conscripted a battle troll to fight for them. Fully armed and armored, the troll unleashed a terrifying roar as it came crashing through the crowd to attack young Barnabas. The brute beast had no conscience to appeal to, and thus no chance for redemption, so Barnabas ran towards the oncoming beast at full speed. Barnabas leapt 8 feet into the air, swinging the sword of power. Never having been charged at by any person before, the troll was too surprised and too slow to react. The blade cut right through the iron neck band of the creature and followed through to sever its head from its body. Barnabas cried out: "Warriors of darkness, do you now yield to accept a just judgment, or do you choose to die fighting. At this point I am inclined to accept one more than the other, so I suggest you choose quickly, and you choose wisely."

Such was their hatred and their fury that they obeyed the voice of their soggy captain who had climbed back onto the pier and screamed at them to kill the challenger. With swift movements, they simultaneously drew their swords and advanced on Barnabas who charged into the midst of them as flashes of lightning shot from his raised weapon. Only the foolish dared strike at him, as each attacker was easily repelled and knocked off his feet. While still surrounded, Barnabas sheathed his sword and said,

"Enough of this, we accept your surrender."

The few soldiers still remaining on their feet turned their sword hilts to the now unarmed Barnabas and set their swords on the pier.

The crew of the Karu Mar and the villagers all shouted for joy, and from that day forward the day was celebrated as a holiday.

As Captain Eli noticed some of the villagers were screaming for vengeance against the now captured soldiers, he intervened:

"Deal justly with these Herzlos who have surrendered. If you abuse them while they are unarmed in your power, you will prove yourselves no different than them. What they have just seen has shaken their warrior world to its core. They have been confronted by the fact that the power of the Old Kingdom has returned and that higher power showed them mercy. They are also honor bound to the warrior who could have killed them all but showed them mercy. Still, the truth is, not all of them will fare well and their captain will likely disappear and try to find a way to join himself with some evil somewhere at the first chance. Maintain guard on them here until I prepare my ship to transport them back to their homeland.

# Fondest Farewells

E li gathered his crew together for a final farewell:

"I am leaving now, but not without a thankful heart for the joy and the fellowship we have shared. I thank you, my friends, for everything. When the time is right, I will return. If you then choose to join me for the final battle, then I will be glad for your company. If you choose to stay, I will understand, but it will be you who will lose the joy of victory; you will only see it from the side. Time will tell. Time is short. Live for the kingdom, the kingdom come, may justice rule."

All the crew members bid farewell to Captain Eli and Clarence, who would continue on as his cook. Rohani and Sadik approached the stern of the ship and lovingly said good-bye to Adalet, wishing her a peaceful journey. Still, neither

Rohani nor Sadik knew of the presence of Kaga-yaku with her.

Rohani told her, "You also have Blue and Clarence to keep you companion as you sail to meet Melissa.

Sadik chimed in and said, "She is a lovely girl and you two will become the best of friends, I know."

Before the prisoners were loaded on the ship, Adalet was safely and securely hidden in the captain's cabin, where she would remain until the Herzlos departed at the first stop, just a few days' sail away.

Eli stood at the helm of the Karu Mar. The mooring ropes dropped, and the ship sailed swiftly, silently out to sea as Captain Eli gave them one last wave in the distance, he momentarily dipped the ship's flags to honor them.

"When do you think we will see him again?" Sadik asked Rohani.

"I have no idea, but I do know it will be at the right time, even if it won't be in the best of times until the present is restored to the past so this place can have its originally intended future."

Sadik traced Rohani's timeline back and forth with his fingers. It took him a while to fully replay Rohani's last statement and understand it, but then he replied, "You have quite the way with words, my four-legged, angel- befriended friend."

The day of the town's emancipation from the rule of the Herzlos was celebrated as an annual event with parades and many festivities. Every one of the crew members was financially blessed beyond their wildest dreams from their share of the unrestored treasures.

Once the soldiers of Toh-Kali had returned to their homeland, stories of Captain Eli and his crew were told and many were influenced. Those who had the heart to do so searched the prophecies and some called for a return to the Old Kingdom.

# Readiness Training

C aptain Eli, Blue, Adalet and the hidden Kagayaku were now on their own on the voyage to deliver Adalet to be cared for by Melissa's aunt and Captain Horace. Eli invited Adalet to come topside to talk with him: "Oh, and bring Kagayaku with you when you come. Yes, I know about your little glowing friend – we have much to talk about."

All during the voyage, Captain Eli shared with them of the history of the land of Lusa, of its beauty and harmony, and its tragic fall. Tears filled his eyes as he shared how Lusa was once a perfectly peaceful kingdom until the rebellion of self-centeredness divided the Lusans, the animals and the dragons, and evil was propagated. Eli informed them:

"We are in the last chapter of the book before the new beginning. Adalet and Kagayaku, you have been chosen to play an important role in unifying the forces of good and restoring justice. Kagayaku, Fred sends his greetings and looks forward to watching you aid in the restoration of the kingdom. You are still young, but it is incumbent upon you to share with Adalet all that you know of the power of light and harmony. Teach her how to channel the energies that you channel, as best as a non-Umeme can." Eli continued:

"Adalet, though you are yet a young girl now, I know there is a deep calling in your heart, a destiny to follow, for you are destined for greatness. This responsibility comes with it a call to absolute discipline and total humility. Now, both of you, celebrate life fully and freely, and always keep a thankful heart, but also be always growing in the power of the kingdom, and be ready to defend all that is pure and in need of protection. Most important of all, remember that your strength lies in your love for what is good, not in your hatred of what is evil. Power flows greatest through the one with the purest love."

They all enjoyed a peaceful sail to Hang-gu, and Eli and Horace had a wonderful visit there. Melissa was fully restored to health; in fact, she was now stronger and more agile than she was before her sickness, and she continued to grow stronger. She and Adalet became instant friends and had a great sisterly love for one another.

As promised, Malpirius returned to take Melissa for a ride, and Adalet joined her on the amazing flight. As they were flying along, Adalet was amazed at the strength of the great dragon, and a thought came to her: "I wonder if this dragon could help me find and free my parents from Prince Toh-Kali?"

When they were finished with their flight, the dragon spoke to Adalet alone and told her he perceived she was destined to be a warrior princess to fight along with him and the good dragons. He told her:

"Yes, my young princess, I am ready and willing to help in the rescue of your parents, but you must continue your training with Kagayaku (yes, I know of your glowing friend)."

"When the time is right, I will come to get you and we shall fight together to restore the kingdom. Take care, my princess, I shall return in due time. I leave you with this final secret: you have been chosen, but so has your young friend Melissa. This is most important; she is not to know the true source of her healing and strength, for it could confuse her, and there is more power in the secrecy of this truth than in its telling." The dragon continued:

"Study the way of the dragons, for you both must train in our way. I am entrusting you with one of the deepest secrets on this entire planet. You will begin to see unique powers developing within Melissa as you both learn from Kagayaku. Know this, but you must never reveal to her or anyone else that the healing power of the fire flower that restored her came from the blood of a chosen dragon, and that power now resides in her heart and flows in her veins. When the time is right, that power will come to fullness and the Old Kingdom will be restored.

Later that day Malpirius bid farewell to them all and flew away. Then, all too soon, it was time for Eli and Blue to bid them good-bye and sail to yet more adventures. A continent away, Prince Toh-Kali's Black Ship was sailing into an ocean cave that led deep into a dark mountain that was enshrouded in mist. A great sea monster known as a Zirakuni guarded the only navigable harbor entrance to this forbidding island. Flashes of fire appeared in the middle of the clouds as multiple dragons were seen circling the peak. Distant drums were calling up an assembly of unholy warriors that were preparing for the battle to ensure that darkness ruled the land. The upcoming battle would determine the fate of the land of Lusa.

# Alphabetical Index of Characters, Places

(Words are literal or derivations, but the theme of universality remains central)

**Adalet –** Turkish for justice. Young daughter of Isihe and Roonaan, the just and noble rulers who are kidnapped by Prince Toh-Kali when their ship is attacked and sunk at sea. Adalet survives thanks to her friend Kagayaku. She is a major player in book II.

**Arasibo –** Chief on the Corbatanos. Alteration of Arecibo, a coastal city in Puerto Rico.

**Bartholomew –** Hebrew (son of a farmer) and Barnabas (son of encouragement) (AKA the Do-gooders) Father/son who sailed with Eli from the isle of Mekaikki.

**Black Dragon –** King of Dragons who was deposed and isolated himself after the other dragons joined together in the war that divided the Lusans.

**Blue** – a giant greenish octopus who befriends the crew of the Karu Mar and accompanies them on their adventures.

**Captain Eli** – protagonist. The one who comes to restore the peace and unity of the Old Kingdom in the land of Lusa.

**Captain Horace** – The Librarian, grandfather of Melissa. The name Horace is related to "Timekeeper".

**Chara** – Greek for joy/gladness

**Chief of the Boat (COB or Chief)** - The sheriff from Mekaikki. Principal character.

**Clarence** - the ship's cook

**Corbatanos** – a play on words concerning a sad part of history. Corbata means necktie in Spanish. The Taino natives were tortured and enslaved by the Spaniards in the conquering of Puerto Rico, although it was for gold and not for silver. Their story reflects the imprisonment of natives in Mexico and South America in the heartless pursuit of silver and gold.

**Ei en no ai –** Japanese for eternal love. Tidal pools in which the Umemes live. (Pronounced A en no eye)

**Fred –** Derived from Old Norse word for peace, protection – Angelic being, friend and protector of Captain Eli.

**Hang-gu –** Korean for harbor (Island where Captain Horace, Melissa, and later Adalet lived).

**Herzlos –** German word for heartless

**Huba Amal –** derivation of Arabic for love of money, Sadik's business partner

**Isihe –** Zulu/Swahili for mercy. The mother of Adalet and good queen who was kidnapped. (Pronounced Ish hey)

**Jin Jiang –** Chinese for goldsmith. Minor character with no role.

**Jeffery,** son of Grumpy Old Bill, original crew members from Mekaikki.

**Kagayaku –** Japanese for "glowing". The name of the Umeme that befriended Adalet.

**King of Dragons –** Black Dragon who substantiates Eli's prophetic calling. The Black Dragon will feature in the final battle in Book II.

**Karu Mar –** Karu - Hindu/Sanskrit for singer, poet, maker + Mar - Spanish for sea. Captain Eli's ship.

**Kormilar –** Croatian for helmsman. He accompanies Sideros on a ship that is wrecked on an island.

**Librarian –** aka Captain Horace

**Lusa –** Derivation of Spanish word luz for light. The planet on which the characters live.

**Malpirius –** Created word. Mal, meaning bad + pyro meaning fire. The great Red Dragon that betrayed the Old Kingdom and allied with Prince Toh-Kali. Eli restores Malpirius to work to build the Old Kingdom. He will play a role in book II.

**Mashal –** Hebrew word for example. A dragon that gives his life to save another, which is a central element in the balance of power between good and evil in the land of Lusa.

**Mekaikki –** Finnish for 'All of Us or rest of us', the island where Eli picks most of his crew.

**Melissa –** Grand daughter of Captain Horace. She is saved from a deadly illness by the power of the fire flower, which grew over the grave of Mashal. She is a major player in Book II.

**Nagos –** Potawatomi Native American word for star

**Margala –** A small, roundish dragon like creature. An orphaned Nargala, Quiz, joins the crew.

**Old Bill –** A "grumpy" old Lusan who has a good heart. Father of Jeffery. They joined Eli on Mekaikki.

**Panday –** Filipino word for Blacksmith. Travels with Captain Eli. In the Philippines, there is still an unfortunate degree of prejudice against blacks.

**Perak –** Malay for silver. Minor character, no role.

**Rohani -** Indonesian for spiritual, spiritually sensitive, noetic, name for the burro.

**Roonaan –** Somali for kindness. Good king, father of Adalet and husband to Isihe.

**Sadik –** Arabic for honest, sincere. The Chimono, a principal character throughout the book.

**Sideros –** Greek for iron. He is the runaway son of Panday, the blacksmith.

**Toh-Kali -** Lakota word for enemy. Prince of Reitans. Principal antagonist.

**Kohatu Wakawa -** Maori for Stone of Judgment, A stone that gives authority to rule over dragons, makes the bearer impervious to dragon fire.

**Umeme –** Swahili for fluorescence/lightning/electricity. It is a being of light named Kaga-yaku that befriends Adalet, protects her, and trains her to fight alongside her against Prince Toh-Kali's forces in Book II. (Pronounced oo meh meh)

**Visala –** Nepali word for gigantic. Silver miners with whom the Corbatanos once traded.

**Yamba Kusamvana –** combine two words Begin and Conflict in the Paiute language. Alternate name the dragons call Mashal's Island.

**Yunqui –** A name derived from El Yunque, a mountain in Puerto Rico – a young ship-wrecked sailor who stays on an island and marries a native girl. (Pronounced Yoonkee)

**Zirakuni –** Kiowa Native American for water monster